I0591611

THE FAERIE GIRL AND OTHER TALES

Six Magical Stories

ANTHEA SHARP

Fiddlehead Press

Want to make sure you hear about Anthea's new books? Join her newsletter, and get a *free* short story when you sign up! Find out more at www.antheasharp.com

Cover by Ravven

Professional editing by LH Temple, Ellen Campbell, Crystal Watanabe. Copyediting by Editing720.

ISBN: 9781680130249

QUALITY CONTROL: We care about producing error-free books. If you discover a typo or formatting issue, please contact antheasharp@hotmail so that it may be corrected.

For all the hidden and fey girls - you know who you are-

CONTENTS

The Faerie Girl   1
The Sea King's Daughter   20

BREA'S TALE

1. Waterborne   61
2. Passage   77
3. Arrival   95

The Faerie Invasion   123
Goblin in Love   145
The Tree of Fate and Wishes   157

Other Works   175
About the Author   177

THE FAERIE GIRL

COUNTY WICKLOW, Ireland, Summer 1845

The first time Colin Barrington saw the wild girl, he knew she was a faerie.

He crouched in the bushes of the Vinewood—that part of the Barrington estate deliberately left untamed—and tried to breathe as silently as possible. The air smelled of leaves and water. Thorns pricked the backs of his hands, and his trousers were damp and muddy at the knees.

He would have to sneak back into the manor in order to avoid stern words from his tutor. Since he was nearly thirteen now it would be the cane for him as well, should Mr. Pembroke catch him. But Colin did not care one whit. He would trade a dozen canings for this single glimpse of the faerie girl.

She knelt at the edge of the small pond hidden in the heart of the woods. Her bare arms and legs poked, thin as sticks, from a garment made of cobwebs and mist. Dark hair tangled about her sharp features, concealing her ears—but he was certain their tips tapered into points. He could not see her wings, but that did not matter overmuch. Not every type of faerie had wings, or perhaps she'd concealed them with some enchantment, making them invisible to human eyes.

To a casual onlooker, the girl might appear human, but Colin knew better. His old nurse had told him the stories before she'd passed on, stories of the Fair Folk, the Wee People who inhabited the secret places of Eire.

"Airrreh? Where's that?" he'd asked.

Nurse had laughed and pulled him close, her arm warm about his shoulders. "Ah, *mo chroi*, it is this very land. What you English call Ireland. 'Tis thick with the magic of old."

Her words ringing in his ears, Colin held his breath. At last, he himself had discovered that hidden magic.

A leaf drifted from one of the sycamores and landed, a lazy golden boat, on the surface of the pond. The faerie girl bent forward, her pale, dirt-streaked hands resting on her knees. She stared intently down into the water.

Then she began to sing.

It was a song full of hushing and pebbles, in a language Colin half-remembered. Nurse had used to sing thus. Realization flashed through him, white-hot. Why, his old nurse had been a faerie herself! How else could she have known the fey lullabies she crooned to him? This feral creature before him sounded much the same, her song like cool polished stones, a sound that that pulled at his middle.

Without meaning to, Colin leaned closer. The bush he was crouched behind rustled, and he froze.

The girl did not look at him, but one corner of her mouth curled into a sly smile, tilted like a sickle moon. Slowly, still singing, she slid her hands into the pond. The dark water barely rippled as she submerged her arms up to the elbow.

One moment there was stillness, and the pale reflection of the faerie's face. Then the water broke into splash and sparkle as she pulled up a fish, a small, struggling trout that thrashed and beat the pond with its tail.

"Put it back!" Colin was instantly on his feet, confronting the girl.

His pulse raced, frantic as the fish. Would she flee now, back to her enchanted world, or perhaps cast some evil spell over him?

The faerie set the fish on the bank and held it there with one hand, then cocked her head and looked at him. Her eyes were dark, dark brown. They looked old in her young face.

"Nay." Her voice had a strange lilt, the word coming out more like *nigh*.

"It's my fish," Colin said. "I command you to return it to the water."

A stray sunbeam fell slantwise through the trees, illuminating the trout's slick scales, the trickle of blood from beneath one gill. He could not bear to watch as it flopped and strained, dying there beneath the girl's hand.

"Yer lordship's fish?" She smiled, sharp and defiant. "Nay, tis mine now, caught fairly."

Colin had to listen carefully to recognize her words, twined as they were in the knotwork of her accent.

"What do you want with a fish?" he asked.

It had stilled now, its eye filming over with death. Too late for him to insist she throw it back into the water.

Her eyes widened above the hollows of her cheeks, then she gave a bitter-edged laugh. "Want with it? Why, it's my supper, poor mouthful though it might be."

"Raw?" He took a step back. Nurse had always told him the Fair Folk were dangerous and unpredictable, but he had never imagined them to be so savage.

"If need be." She shrugged and scooped up the trout.

"But why eat it at all? I thought you lived on nectar and cakes."

Or something of the sort. His nurse had warned him to beware of any food or drink offered by the faeries. It seemed odd that this creature would desire mortal food.

Her eyes narrowed to dark slits. "Easier, is it, believing such things up at the Big House? What a fine tale you spin, yer lordship."

She rose smoothly to her feet, her bare toes smudged with mud.

"Stop calling me that. My name's Colin." Too late he recalled he should never give the Fair Folk his true name. Now she would have power over him.

But perhaps he had some in return.

"You may keep the fish," he said. "But you owe me for it, as it was taken from my land."

She regarded him from her ancient eyes for a long moment. Colin felt as though she stared right through him, past the fine linen of his shirt to his heart, beating hot and uncertain in his chest.

"Me name's Siofra," she said.

Shee-frah. He turned the unfamiliar syllables silently in his mouth. It was a fitting name for a faerie girl.

Between one blink and the next, she disappeared. The branches rustled and he caught a blur of grey beyond, but Siofra was gone. A thrush sang, liquid and lonely from the top of the sycamore, underscoring the silence of the wood. Had he imagined her?

But the ground beside the pond was damp, an iridescent smear of scales visible on the dark earth of the bank.

That evening, the cook served fish for dinner—a massive halibut covered in rich sauce.

Colin wondered if Siofra had eaten her fish raw. Or, indeed, if she'd eaten it at all. Likely she'd simply been toying and teasing with him, the way the Fair Folk were said to do.

He sat across from his mother at the long dining table. His father, the third Earl of Barrington, presided at the head. Candles burned in polished silver candelabra, illuminating the food, though evening light still sifted in through the mullioned windows. Colin had only recently been allowed to dine with his parents, in practice for meeting others in society when he was sent off to Eton that fall.

"Lovely weather for riding, today," Lord Barrington said.

"Yes," Colin's mother said, her voice soft as usual. "I saw you go out with Jones. And how is the estate faring?"

It was Wednesday, the usual day for his father and the estate manager to go about their rounds. For a moment, Colin thought he might mention seeing Siofra, then quickly swallowed the notion. A poor showing that would make, bringing fairy tales to the table when he was expected to be growing up into a proper young man.

Lord Barrington's expression darkened. "The tenant's crops are failing, Maud. It will be a grim autumn if this continues—and a worse spring, should there be no seed potatoes."

"Failing?" Colin asked.

"A blight, rotting the potatoes in the ground." His father

sighed heavily. "They cannot pay their rents when they can scarce feed themselves."

"I will take some bread around to the cottages tomorrow," Lady Barrington said. "Though I do believe God is punishing them for their Papist ways."

Colin was a bit unclear on what that meant, though he knew better than to ask his mother. Something to do with God, at any rate, and not young boys.

"Take two of the footmen with you and stay clear of the woods," Lord Barrington said. "There's a group of tinkers in the area."

Colin's mother dropped her gaze to her plate of barely eaten food. "Might we not return to England, Johnathan? Ireland is so barbaric."

She gave a tiny shudder.

"You have endured it well enough these last dozen years. And it is a healthy place to raise our children. Look at our Colin, there. Why, the lad is nearly as tall as myself."

Colin smiled over at his father. He wished he could change places with his mother, and stay behind while she went merrily off to England. No matter what she said, this was home, not that country across the Irish Sea where he'd never set foot. He belonged in Ireland. In *Eire*.

The next day he went to the heart of the Vinewood and sat silently beside the still pond, but there was no sign of the faerie maiden. The water shivered with the wind, and more boats made of leaves eddied on the surface, but there was no wild Siofra stealing his trout.

He returned the next afternoon, caring little for his neglected schoolwork.

This time he was rewarded. He'd schooled himself to move quietly over the soft loam, whispering past the underbrush, and so he heard her before he saw her.

She was sitting beside the water and singing again, the wild syllables spilling from her lips. He hesitated by the rough trunk of an oak tree, fingers gripping the wood, until she finished her song and looked up at him. Again she gave him that sly glance.

"Well, 'tis the young lordling creeping about. Here to keep me from taking one of your silver trout?"

"No." He approached her slowly, afraid of startling her into flight. "I've brought you something."

Her dark eyes narrowed. "Think you to be tricking me?"

"Of course not." He drew himself up. "I am an honorable man."

"Oh, aye." Laughter silvered her voice as she rose, her bare feet covered with mud. "Honorable like all your kind, taking the land, starving the people, making your way over broken backs and bones."

They were faerie words, incomprehensible, but he still felt a strange, confused guilt nestle under his ribcage. This close he could taste her scent—smoke and something acrid he had no name for, like bitter herbs.

He pulled a packet from his pocket and thrust it at here. "Here."

Tilting her head, she regarded the bulky kerchief wrapped with string. "What is it?"

"A book. See?" He pulled back a corner of the linen, to reveal the leather cover embossed with gold. "A volume of poems, by Keats. They're quite good."

"A book!" Her body curved over with laughter, her black hair spilling in tangles about her face. "And what good is that, I ask you? I cannot read it."

Embarrassed heat flushed through him. How foolish, to assume a faerie could decipher the King's English. She knew the language of frost and petal, could read patterns in the stars. What use had she for a mortal book?

He began to slip it back into his pocket but she darted forward, quick as a breath of wind, and snatched it from him. Before he could react, she returned to the pond's edge, several arm-lengths away.

"There are pictures," he offered. "I didn't mean to insult you."

"Next time bring something useful, like food. Or coin."

"I will."

The words had no sooner left his mouth than she was gone, a flicker of white dancing away through the shadowed woods. Despite her dismissive tone, she'd taken the book with her.

Colin indulged in a brief imagining of Siofra perched on a toadstool beneath a sky full of unknown stars, paging through the book by the light of the moon. He hoped the pictures would bring her some pleasure, though the words might be meaningless.

❧

She was waiting for him the next day, seated on a mossy log near the edge of the pond. As soon as he stepped out of the woods, her gaze fixed on him, her eyes bright above her sharp cheekbones.

"Good afternoon," he said, carefully settling on the end of the log, far enough that he would not frighten her. He hoped.

His trousers would bear stains from the damp moss and dirt, but he didn't care. Although perhaps he should. His tutor would be bearing tales to Lord Barrington about his wayward son, but Colin did not know if he would ever again have the chance to converse with a faerie. It was worth the inevitable punishment.

"What did you bring?" She eyed the sack he'd slung over his shoulder.

"Coin, and food. And something more. Wait," he said as she reached for it. "You must give me something in return."

Her expression turned wary, and she leaned away from him, her bare toes flexing into the soil. He could feel her tensing to flee.

"Stay! I won't harm you. I won't even touch you. I promise, on my honor as a gentlemen."

She gave a delicate snort, but settled back upon her mossy perch. "The promise of a foreign lordling upon this soil means nothing. Words are empty sounds, and honor can be twisted to any end."

"That's not true. The gentleman's code is absolute. As a future lord, I will always follow truth and honor. It is my duty."

The doubt in her face shook him. But she was a faerie. What did she know of such things?

"And is it an honorable thing to sneak away from your responsibilities each afternoon?" she asked, a mocking lift to her brow. "Is it a truthful thing to take a book from your father's library and give it away without asking?"

His chest tightened. "That's different."

"'Tis not." She tilted her head. "Men make excuses for the things they do. Especially lords."

"If all you can do is insult me, then I'll just be going." He rose, fingers clutched around the neck of his sack.

Sunlight shone lazy through the branches, and a small brown bird hopped along a nearby branch, but his heart was hot with shame. With longing. He wanted to stay, but her words stung him almost unbearably.

"Sit," she said. "I don't mean to offend."

Perhaps she was lying, but there was a hint of remorse in her face. Enough that he took a deep breath and sat again upon the log. The seat of his trousers were damp, and he noticed a smear of mud across one knee.

"Now," she continued. "What was it you were wanting in return for that wee sack?"

"I want..." He swallowed, hoping she would not continue to mock him. "I want you to teach me that song. The one you were singing the first time I saw you."

Surprise flashed through her eyes, a spark of silver, but her expression did not turn to scorn. Much to his relief.

"A song, is it?" she asked. "What would such as you want with a song?"

He shrugged, though the answer burned inside him. *Magic. Mystery.* An escape from the humdrum world of a young lord-to-be.

"Will you teach me?"

She gave him a long, level look. "Can you sing?"

His nurse used to tell him he had a fine, strong voice, and in church he could always cleave to the melody of the hymns. Although... if he learned a faerie song, would the words scorch his mouth? Was it ungodly?

Colin shook off his doubts. "I can sing," he declared.

"Well then. I'll teach you, and after that you'll give me yon sack."

The bargain struck, she slid closer to him on the log, though not so close that he might reach and touch her.

Straddling their perch, she faced him, her bare knees putting him in mind of pale mushrooms poking up through the loam.

"The melody first," she said. "Hum it now, like this."

For a moment he closed his eyes, letting the sound of her voice weave through him. The tune was a simple, twining thing, like vines curling about a branch, or the eddies of current in a clear, cool stream.

After she'd hummed it through twice, he joined her, his voice lower and a bit husky, but not so bad a match to her sweet tones. He prayed his voice would not crack as it sometimes did, making the melody leap like an alarmed hare before the hounds.

To his relief, his throat behaved. He hummed more strongly, feeling the shape of the music press against his mouth.

"Good," she said after they had hummed it seven times through. "Now the words."

There was laughter in her voice, and he understood why when he began to try and mimic her hushing, gurgling syllables. It was the language of water and rock, of forest and fen—nothing that came naturally to his tongue. He mangled the words dreadfully, until she waved at him to stop.

"I'll tell you the meaning of the song," she said. "Perhaps t'will help."

He feared nothing would, but he sat, letting the wind ruffle his hair and the dappled light play across his fingers as she spoke.

"Tis a lullaby, telling children to close their eyes and sleep," she said. "For on the roof of the house there are bright faeries, playing and drinking under the gentle rays of the spring moon."

The words blended with the stillness of the clearing, and he imagined the bright faeries creeping closer to listen.

"Here they come to call the child out," she continued softly. "Wishing to draw him into the faery mound. Hushabye, hush. You're not to go with them."

Colin's skin prickled. It was, indeed, a song of faerie magic.

"Try now," Siofra said.

"Show heen," he sang, trying to make his voice catch in the back of his throat, the way hers did. "Show hoe."

"Better." She gave him her slantways smile. "Again."

Finally, when the shadows fell long through the trees, she rose.

"Tis a good enough start," she said. "Tomorrow I'll teach you the next part."

"I'll practice," he said, already turning the song over and over in his head. He'd no doubt the strange words would haunt his dreams that night.

"Then we'll meet again, tomorrow." She held out her hand.

For a moment, he thought she was urging him to set his hand in hers, so that she might lead him into the faerie mound. He rose, then belatedly realized she wanted the sack he'd brought.

Tamping down his surge of disappointment, he gave it to her.

"Bread and cheese, and coin," he said. "And a gift."

He hoped she would like the Venetian glass paperweight, though perhaps faeries cared nothing for such things. Still, he'd always been captivated by the whorls of blue and silver floating inside the glass. Indeed, he'd spent so much time studying it where it stood upon his father's desk, that the earl had laughingly given it to him, warning him not to fall into the sphere and be lost forever.

"I won't," he'd said solemnly, clutching the glass to his chest.

It was one of his most precious possessions, but now he had something even more magical. The song.

Siofra tipped her head in thanks, or farewell, then lightly skipped backward, slipped between two oaks, and was gone.

❦

She did not come the next afternoon.

Colin waited until twilight sifted shadows across the sky, but the clearing remained empty. A blue dragonfly hovered for some time over the pond, and a squirrel hopped from branch to branch nearby, but there was no sign of the faerie maid.

He sang the song, the part of it he knew, over and over. First softly, then loudly, hoping the sound of it would call her to him.

Only the birds sang back.

Dispirited, he tromped back through the woods and into the formal gardens, swishing a long stick he'd picked up from the ground. He whacked the heads off a few flowers, but felt no better for it.

The next day she did not appear, either. He waited—first angry, then despondent, until an afternoon rain squall drove him back to the manor house. Drops trickled down his collar from his wet hair, and in the garden the flowers lay flat upon the grass, weighted down with rain.

At dinner, his father gave him a sharp lecture about the scholarly responsibilities of young gentlemen.

"I'll not have you neglecting your schoolwork," the earl said, while Colin's mother looked on with disappointed eyes. "At Eton, you won't be able to shirk, and I won't stand for it now. Do you understand? You will not leave the house without my permission for the rest of the week."

"Yes, sir." Colin poked at the roast beef upon his plate.

He had no appetite, and hated the thought that he would not be free to go to the pond for at least three days. Why had Siofra not come?

"Speaking of furthering your education," his father said, something cold in his tone, "you'll be coming to the village with me tomorrow. There have been reports of thievery, and I've received word that the suspects have been apprehended. The magistrate will pass sentence upon them in the morning, and you and I will go see justice done. It is your duty to attend. And learn."

"Is it the tinkers?" Colin's mother gripped her napkin, her face paling. "They'll murder us in our beds, I'm sure of it. You should never have agreed to let them camp beside the river."

"Do not fear, Gwendolyn." The earl patted his wife's hand. "They've overstayed their welcome. Tomorrow, after the sentences are carried out, they will be gone."

❦

Colin did not want to don his riding clothes and accompany Lord Barrington to the village. Reluctantly he rose and dressed, and after a quiet breakfast, followed his father outside and mounted upon his gelding.

As he trailed his father's horse down the lane, the woods called to him—the leaves shimmering with new light, the still eye of the pond waiting. He wished he could slip away and meet Siofra, but there was no help for it but to go and be a lordling.

As they rode, he let the horse's hoof beats keep rhythm to

the song he sang under his breath. The strange, lush syllables were slowly becoming more familiar against his tongue.

They reached the outskirts of the village soon enough, the cottages gathered together along the main street, with colorful gardens out front and sheds behind for the livestock. Their horse's hooves now rang over cobbles, not the quiet dust of the road. Belatedly, Colin spurred his mount up alongside his father's.

"What did the tinkers steal?" he asked, "and what is their punishment?"

"Two chickens and a quart of gooseberries from Farmer O'Dowd."

"That's not so very terrible, is it?"

The earl gave him a stern look. "Enough to warrant two months' hard labor and a whipping. But that's not the worst of it. One of the Travellers was found to be in possession of items she had no business having."

A cold tendril of dread wrapped around Colin's gut. He tried to keep his expression calm as he glanced up at his father. "What kind of items?"

"A book of poems, and a pretty bauble. Perhaps you know the ones?" Lord Barrington's voice was all hard iron. "They are the property of our estate. I can only assume they were stolen."

"They were *not* stolen," Colin said, his throat dry with fear. His next words would condemn him to a severe beating, perhaps worse, but he could not remain silent. "I gave them away. To a girl."

"So that's what you've been doing instead of attending your schoolwork—conniving with a tinker in the woods." Cold anger shone from his father's eyes. "Giving a worthless chit of a girl two treasures from our very home."

Colin shrank from the earl's expression.

"She's not worthless," he declared. "Nor a tinker. She's a faerie."

"Ha!" The earl's bark of laughter had nothing of humor in it. "You're about to reap the rewards of your unfortunate choices, my boy."

What had he done? His heart pounded painfully against his ribs.

The bright sunshine and cheerfully painted store fronts were at odds with the darkness creeping over him. There was a crowd in the square, gathered in a rough semicircle around the whipping post. Their voices scraped Colin's ears, and he hunched his shoulders.

Siofra couldn't be a mortal girl. She simply couldn't.

Yet there she stood in her scrap of a dress, her wild hair tangled about her face, glaring at the men who held her. Colin swallowed back the bitter taste of disillusionment. She was simply a human girl, after all.

And yet, she still had a fey quality about her, a breath of wildness and starlight. His heart warred with his head, trying to understand.

Lord Barrington halted outside the pub and dismounted, gesturing for Colin to do the same. A hollow-cheeked lad was waiting to take their horses. Bowing low, he did not meet Colin's eyes as he led their mounts away.

A few short days ago, Colin would have taken such deference as his due, but now it gave him pause. The lad was near his own age, his clothing patched at the elbows and knees, his coat sleeves too short for his gangly frame.

"Come," the earl said, striding forward.

The crowd moved back, letting them through, and all too soon Colin and his father stood in front of the whipping post.

The magistrate, looking self-important, held a sheaf of documents, and beside him slouched a burly fellow with a leather whip coiled in his hand.

And to the side of them, Siofra, her dark eyes huge in her pale face. Colin could not bear to look at her.

A man was tied to the post, his bare back gleaming with sweat in the sunlight. Beyond him, on the edge of the crowd, stood the Travellers—identifiable both by the mix of fear and defiance on their faces and the wide berth the townspeople gave them.

The magistrate held up his hand, and the crowd quieted.

"Johnny Black, guilty of stealing two fowl and a quart of berries from Mr. O'Dowd's farm. Ten lashes and three months' hard labor on the roads."

The crowd murmured, and the Travellers stirred restlessly, but no one denied Johnny Black's guilt or spoke out against the punishment.

The whip rose, then fell with a harsh slap against the man's back. He twitched in pain, but did not cry out. After the second lash, Colin looked away. Nausea built in his throat as he counted the strokes. By the sixth lash, the man was groaning, and by the eighth he cried out with every stroke.

After what felt an eternity, the whipping ended. Two women rushed to the post and, the moment Johnny Black's hands were untied, carefully helped him upright. Blood smeared his back, and seven red droplets splashed on the cobbles.

"You may tend him," the magistrate said, "but in the gaol. His labor begins tomorrow."

One of the women stared defiantly and began to speak, but her companion hissed sharply. There was no mercy here.

Colin's mind shied from what was to come. Despite

himself, he glanced at Siofra, standing pale and exceedingly thin beside the whipping post. Her dark eyes met his, and he thought he saw a flash of silver in their depths.

"Sarah Casey," the magistrate announced. "Ten lashes and six months' hard labor in the Ballyclare Quarry for stealing items valued at over forty pounds from the Barrington Estate."

"She did not!" Colin cried.

"Silence." His father's hard hand encircled Colin's arm. "I'll not have the family name besmirched in this matter. The girl is a thief."

The crowd looked at them, murmuring, and in that second of distraction Siofra slid free of the men holding her—a flash of white, and skinny limbs. In the heartbeat before she disappeared into the crowd, he swore she winked at him.

"Stop her!" the magistrate bellowed.

"Ten pounds to anyone who apprehends the girl," Lord Barrington called out.

His words made the crowd turn and scurry, and Colin tensed, waiting for the terrible moment that someone would yell that they'd caught Siofra.

That moment did not come.

The Travellers slowly melted away while the villagers searched, turning over wheelbarrows and sending their children running all about the town. After half an hour of standing in the square and watching the fruitless activity, Lord Barrington gave an impatient growl.

"They will find her," he said. "It does us no good to watch. The magistrate will notify me the moment the girl is caught."

His angry steps were sharp against the cobbles as he strode back to the pub to retrieve their horses. Colin followed, his heart half shadowed in despair, half bright with hope.

In the fall, Colin Barrington entered Eton. His back bore the thin welts of scars from the beating his father had given him—made more severe by the fact that the tinker girl was never found.

Every summer until he reached his majority he returned to the Barrington Estate, learning the management of the earldom. He spoke little, but helped where he could as the hunger spread across the land. After his father died, he took the earl's seat in the Irish Parliament, advocating for better conditions for the native populace and less strict punishments for crimes committed by children.

And if the servants at the estate thought it odd that their master would slip away some afternoons to the pond in the Vinewood, and if any heard the sounds of an old song issuing from the woods, they never remarked upon it.

Nor did they mention the lonely look in Colin Barrington's eyes as he returned to his manor, walking slowly through the formal gardens as evening lay like a dove's gray wing across the sky. The only witness to the low sigh of his heart was a dusting of stars, and the sickle moon on the horizon; a spring moon, sharp and slanted as a faerie girl's smile.

Author's Note: The song Síofra teaches Colin is the traditional Gaelic lullaby *Seoithín, seo hó*, taken from the singing of Joe Heaney. Thanks to Sean Williams for giving me the song, and the history. All errors of translation are my own.

THE SEA KING'S DAUGHTER

THE SURFACE of the North Sea rolled and ruffled quietly beneath the May wind. In the sky overhead, gulls caught the eddies, calling in high, lonely voices. The rocky shore of Eire rose on the horizon, a dark blur of land before the water stretched away for thousands of miles to the west.

Beneath the waters, the calm beauty of the day mattered little. Pale sunshine filtered down, and further down, to the very halls of the Sea King, where the matters of the world above meant very little. His palace rose from the sea bed, whorls of shell and pearl glowing with iridescence. Four fanciful towers, one for each of his daughters, were decked with banners of woven sea grass that waved in the gentle eddies

The open, curved halls were traversed by fishes and merfolk alike on their way to the throne room for the birthday celebrations of the king's youngest daughter, Muireen.

This was not any birthday, however, but the coming of age Muireen had been waiting years for. Finally she was turning seventeen and would be allowed to rise to the surface for her first glimpse of the mortal world.

Six years earlier, her eldest sister Aila had been the first of them to break the surface of the bright water and see what wonders the world above held.

"Tell us, tell us," her sisters had clamored when she returned, then listened, wide-eyed, to Aila's descriptions of the wheeling birds, the bright sun, the taste of air in her lungs instead of water.

She had even glimpsed a mortal ship riding majestic over the waves, all unaware of the kingdom they traveled over. Although her bodyguard had not allowed her swim any closer, for fear of discovery, Aila had heard singing, and a strange buzzing instrument not known beneath the sea.

The next sister to rise, Dagmar, had shaken her head dismissively upon her return.

"It's gray and cold," she'd said. "Water spits in cold drops from the sky, and the bones of fish float, rotting, in the waves. There is no reason to visit the world above."

"What of the mortals?" Muireen had asked.

"I saw no sign," Dagmar said, flat disinterest in her voice.

When the second-youngest sister made her trip to the surface, she proclaimed it "quiet and a bit boring."

Privately, Muireen vowed that she would swim toward shore. She would stay from dawn to dusk and do everything she could to catch a glimpse of the mortals who inhabited the world of air. Whether or not the guards that would accompany her would allow such a thing was a question she pushed away. Her determination was strong enough to succeed.

For years, Muireen and her sisters had scavenged the ship-wrecks scattered on the ocean floor. But while her older siblings had lost interest, Muireen still was fascinated by the strange objects to be found in the detritus. She could not make heads nor tails of many of the items, but whether they were weapons or decorations or strange tools, they piqued her imagination.

"Why can we not visit the surface more than once a year?" she'd asked her father. "Surely we can learn things from the mortals above."

"No," the Sea King had said, his voice hard. "The only thing they may teach our kind is death and destruction. Our history is filled with tales of murder, the blood of our people staining the currents while they hunted us down without mercy. Once a year is danger enough."

Only the weight of law and custom kept her father from forbidding all merfolk from ever rising to the surface.

Today, though, was her day. Muireen's heart beat faster. Today, she would feel the mystery of the sun on her face, breathe the strangeness of air, hear the sounds of the birds.

And maybe, if luck was with her, she would set her eyes on a mortal.

⚜

Eiric Airgead set his carefully folded nets in his small boat, checked that it was not taking on water, then stepped in and pushed off from the stone jetty. The sky overhead cupped the pearly pre-dawn light, and the village's small harbor was busy with fishermen heading out to make the day's catch. Half the fleet was already gone, their boats patches of darkness over the pewter water.

The sea wind blew Eiric's dark hair about his face, the breeze strong enough for him to raise sail. Quickly, his boat flew out, rocking up and down when he hit the rougher water outside the sheltering curve of the harbor. Behind him, white-washed cottages glowed softly with the dawn over their shoulders. The stone-walled fields and lanes climbed up the hillside, and he could see a half dozen villagers striding up to tend the fields and flocks.

He'd never had the heart of a farmer, himself. The sea always called to him, the waves whispering his name. The village lived by the sea. And died by it, as well—as no doubt would be his own fate.

But while he lived, he'd ride his small boat over the waves, casting his nets beneath the surface to pull up silver shimmering wonders of fishes. He'd sing, and play the tin whistle tucked in his pocket to pass the time. Most of all, he'd know the freedom of the wind and water, the language of current and cloud.

Bright porpoises danced beside his boat, and seals watched him with their large, dark eyes. The huge *Ainmhí Sheoil* moved like a dark shadow below him, but he was wiser than to cast a line for the shark. His boat was too small, his arms too weak.

It took many men in a larger craft to be able to ride out the death run of such a massive fish. Once, one of the village's boats was gone for nearly an entire moon. When they finally returned, they told a harrowing and heroic tale of being dragged far to the north by the basking shark, at last overcoming it, and then making the long journey home. That winter, the village ate well.

Though Eiric fished alone, he contributed enough to the village's stores that he was considered a hard worker, and a good match for any of the lasses. Red-haired Biddy had made it plain she'd welcome him to come courting, but she had a hard edge that Eiric misliked. Perhaps he might instead woo

Orla, who tended her flock of sheep, but she was a quiet girl. Too quiet, mayhap.

Eiric's mother was gone, and his father as well, leaving no one to push him toward a marriage he was not certain he wanted. And so he fished, and played tunes up to the sky, and was content to live alone.

Muireen's sisters combed out her hair and braided it with pearls. They burnished the silver-blue scales of her tail until it glowed, and told her she was as beautiful as the sun slanting through the midsummer waves.

When she was finally ready, her sisters accompanied her to the curved-walled, iridescent throne room. There, the king and all the court had assembled to bid Muireen a safe journey to the surface. After an eternity of toasts and speeches, it was at last time for her departure. The currents swirled, tugging at Muireen's hair and slipping over her scales, whispering *come, come.*

"Don't do anything foolish," her eldest sister said as she embraced Muireen in farewell.

"Princess." An older warrior bowed before Muireen, her silver hair braided tightly against her head. "I am to be your bodyguard today. My name is Ceilp."

"Well met, Ceilp," Muireen said. "And thank you for your escort."

The Sea King beckoned, and she went obediently to float before him. *Soon. So soon.*

"Daughter." The king's strong voice sent ripples through the water surrounding them. "Today you will breathe air for the first time and claim your birthright between the worlds. I call upon the blessing of the sun and moon to protect you. I command the tides and currents to carry you safely to the world above, and back home to us. Go now, and see, but take care not to be seen in return. The safety of our people rests in concealment and caution. Do you understand?"

"Yes, Father." Muireen dipped her head in consent, but she could not contain the racing of her pulse.

Of course she would be careful, but she would not return until she'd at least glimpsed a mortal. She'd waited her entire life to visit the surface.

The king lifted his scepter made of glimmering shells.

"Safe travels to you Muireen, daughter of the sea," he said. "And to you, warrior Ceilp."

The merfolk and water creatures let out a liquid cheer. Muireen clasped her finned fingers together and bowed to her father. Her escort bowed even lower, and finally they were free to go.

It took all Muireen's control to keep herself swimming at the sedate pace required by politeness. Although she wanted to give a mighty sweep of her tail to propel her through the pearly opening of the palace gates, the backwash would disrupt the onlookers. Only children and uncouth swimmers sent disruptive wakes when they swam inside the palace. Certainly no princess of the sea would behave so rudely—even though her blood bubbled through her like air, seeking to rise.

Up, up to the brightness above the waves.

When the palace was a glowing shell behind them, Muireen glanced at her guard.

"Might we swim a bit faster?" she asked, trying to control the impatient twitch of her tailfins.

Ceilp frowned slightly. "Very well. I can see you won't settle until you take your first breath of air."

Muireen didn't hesitate. Stretching her arms ahead of her, fingers spread wide, she thrust her tail up, then down and surged forward. The sea pulled past, strands of kelp waving wildly behind them. Small silver fishes scattered before them and Muireen laughed aloud.

Ceilp kept pace on her right, and though she was not smiling, some joy sparked in her eyes.

Far off and below them the water shaded to indigo, marking the territory of the sea witch. Muireen glanced down and shivered. No one ventured into the witch's domain without a very good reason, and even then such a journey was fraught with peril. She was an unsavory creature who wished nothing but ill upon the mer.

Legend held that once she had been the sea king's lover, but that her ill-humored nature had at last turned him against her. She'd been banished from court and left to dwell in the bitter shadows she preferred, stirring up mischief when she could.

Still, her magic was powerful, and sometimes merfolk in great need turned to her when all other hope was lost.

A shaft of sunlight sifted overhead, lightening the sea to a delicious greeny-blue, and Muireen banished all thought of the sea witch. Today there was no room for dark tales and darker waters. Not when the adventure of a lifetime awaited.

Eiric fished all morning, his nets yielding a fair catch. When the sun neared its zenith, he pulled out a hunk of brown bread and some dried fish to make a meal. As he finished, brushing the crumbs overboard, the breeze freshened from the west.

He shaded his eyes with one hand and looked to the horizon. Clouds smudged the line between sea and sky, and he frowned. Might be a storm brewing, or mayhap just a squall, but a wise fisherman knew when it was time to head for shore.

Glancing back toward the sheltering bulk of Eire, he realized with a stab of dismay that he'd gone quite a distance from land. Sometimes the currents were tricky out of the north, pushing small boats such as his from their paths and out to sea.

He'd been careless, focused on the good fishing and the sparkle of sunlight on the water and paying little heed to the wind and waves carrying him away. Quickly, he stowed his nets, then wrestled with the sail. The wind was stubborn, changing direction as soon as he'd caught it. The sail luffed, sounding suspiciously like it was laughing at him.

"Hush now," he said, trying to soothe the coarse cloth as well as his own mounting unease. "We'll make it to shore soon enough."

At that, the wind died down entirely. Eiric let out a breath. Why did the elements mock him so?

He didn't want to cast his nets or line back out, in case the breeze freshened. To pass the time, he pulled out his tin whistle, the metal warm from where it had rested inside his coat, and began to play.

Perhaps he could coax the wind to rise if he played something sprightly. Fingers flicking over the holes, Eiric spun the bright notes of a jig into the air. The slap of water against the boat kept an arrhythmic counterpoint but, alas, the sky remained still.

He played another jig, then a reel full of flurries and turns, and then a quieter tune, the melody of an old song about a lover lost at sea. He was not a singer, his voice too rough and low, but with the whistle he could sing out, the notes pure and aching.

Something splashed in the waves behind him.

Eiric turned, halting the music, but there was nothing to be seen except a white froth like lace, already dissolving into the blue green waves. Likely it had been a fish leaping, or perhaps a curious seal, drawn by the sound of his music. Still, that didn't explain the prickling between his shoulder blades.

He waited for several breaths, but whatever it was had gone. Still, he resolved to keep a sharp eye on the water. Fishermen who ignored their instincts went soonest to the bottom of the sea.

☼

"Halt," Ceilp said when Muireen was only a few lengths from the enticing glimmer of the surface.

Impatience surging through her, Muireen did as her escort asked. Overhead, the bottoms of the waves beckoned.

"Why?" she asked.

Ceilp gave her a serious look. "You have never breathed air before. And although our mer magic should make air no different than water, sometimes the transition can be awkward."

"I know," Muireen said. "We must take in a long sip of seawater, then let it out in three quick puffs, then rise to the surface and not breathe in for three heartbeats."

"Indeed." Ceilp said. "Remember it well. Also, it helps to be touching someone who has breathed both air and water. It aids the magic for some reason. Wait." She held out her hand to stay Muireen, who could not seem to keep herself from floating up.

"I will rise first to make sure it is safe," the guard said. "Stay two tail lengths below. Once I determine all is well, rise and take my hand. Then we will break the surface together."

Muireen nodded, her pulse racing like a high tide under the mysterious moon.

With a last, stern look, Ceilp swam up, her tail strokes leaving swirls in the current. After what felt an eon, she descended to where Muireen.

"It is safe," she said. "A storm brews in the distance, but that will not concern us."

She held out her hand, the webs between her fingers a pale orange that echoed the burnished hues of her tail. Muireen folded her fingers around Ceilp's and, tails beating the water, they rose.

In her excitement, Muireen nearly forgot to suck in her seawater and let it out in three pulses. Still, she managed, releasing the last bit of liquid just before the top of her head touched that magical, permeable ceiling where water meets air.

Then her whole face emerged. Conscious of the change in her lungs, she held her breath. Her pulse thundered through her body. Once, twice, thrice. Then she opened her mouth and let the air come in, filling the places that had known only salt and the sea.

The world above the ocean was cool and bright. It felt strange to lose the comforting presence of the water against her skin. Her cheeks and lips and eyes felt bare in a way they never had before, as though something had been peeled away, leaving her exposed.

Her hair was stuck against her head, clinging to her shoulders instead of floating free. And the sounds! Everything was sharp and exciting: the hiss and rush of the water, a high whistling that must be the wind, a distant rumble of surf on stone. The cries of the gulls overhead cut through her.

"Ha!" She could not help her shout of laughter.

"Are you breathing correctly?" Ceilp asked, watching Muireen closely.

"Yes." The word trembled on Muireen's lips. Even her voice was different here, lower and husky-sounding.

"Good." Ceilp released her hand. "Welcome to the world above."

Muireen spun herself in a circle, taking it in. The birds overhead darted and wheeled like fish in the sky. Strange diaphanous whiteness floated higher in the blue. The sun was too strong to look at, the glossy, hard light on the waves enough to make her squint and blink.

"What is that?" She pointed in the direction the sun rose, where a long, dark shape lay low on the horizon.

"Land," Ceilp's said. "The place where humans dwell."

Muireen's new-found breath hitched in excitement. "Can we—"

"No." The older mer's tone was forbidding. "No good comes from anything mortal."

"And what is over there?" Murieen nodded in the opposite direction, where a dark haze filled part of the sky.

"That is the look of a storm blowing in. Fear not; we will be safely below before it arrives."

Muireen frowned. "But I want to see the stars, and the moon, without lengths of water between me and the sky. Surely that is not too much to ask?"

"My duty is to keep you safe, princess." Ceilp emphasized the last word, reminding Muireen of her station, and responsibilities. "For now, you ought to practice changing from breathing air to water, so that your body may become used to the sensation. I will keep watch."

With a sigh, Muireen dove beneath the surface. The water

wrapped about her like a blanket, comforting, yet almost smothering. She longed to throw it off, to rise and feel the excitement of air about her once again.

What would it be like, to live as a human, wholly above the surface? To be unable to breathe water, to move about on two ungainly stalks, trapped against the ground?

She would never know.

Instead, she distracted herself with chasing a nearby school of porpoise in and out of the waves. Ceilp even joined in as they leaped and dove. Each time Murieen broke the barrier between water and air, she took in great breaths, tasting salt and cold and, once, a hint of something wild and green blown off the land.

"What is the land called?" she asked Celip, once the guard seemed in a better mood.

"I've heard it is called Eire," Ceilp said.

"Air?" Muireen laughed. "It is a fitting name."

Ceilp shook her head, but there was warmth in her eyes. "It has a different spelling, and a different nuance on the tongue. It is the name for an ancient goddess of the land, and the mortals have called their home accordingly."

Once again, Muireen glanced at the dark length of the island and silently rolled the name on her tongue. Eire. It seemed a little closer than when she'd first glimpsed it upon the horizon, and she was determined to edge closer still.

After a time the porpoises tired of playing, but under pretext of the chase Muireen had managed to maneuver herself and Ceilp nearer to the land. She sculled idly in the waves, letting the breeze explore her face. Then something tickled the edge of her hearing—a bright, breathy fall of melody that tugged her soul. Music?

"Do you hear that?" She lifted her head. "Oh, Ceilp, might we go a bit closer?"

The older mer set her hands on the two forked daggers belted about her waist, as if to reassure herself of their presence. She glanced up at the sky.

"Music means humans," she said. "It is too dangerous."

"Please?" Muireen tried to keep her yearning from showing in her voice. "We'll be careful. Just—can't we see where it's coming from?"

This was her chance to see a human! She could not turn away from the opportunity.

"No." From Ceilp's tone, there would be no changing her mind.

Muireen shot a regretful glance at the receding porpoises. They would not provide cover any long, which meant she must seize her opportunity now.

Before her guard could guess what she was about, Muireen dipped beneath the waves and sped in the direction the music had come from, using every trick of speed she knew. Behind her, Ceilp called for her to stop, but Muireen ignored the words.

Closer, closer, until she could hear the notes even beneath the waves, wavering and distorted, falling down like tarnished coins. She shivered with delight. Such a sound, made of breath and mystery, was never heard in the sea kingdom. Just ahead, she saw the curved bottom of a small boat, a promise of adventure riding the waves. Barely slowing, she shot up to the surface.

She rose above the waves long enough to glimpse a slender, dark-haired man leaning against the thin mast of his boat, a length of metal held to his lips.

Then Ceilp grabbed her tail and tugged her down with a splash.

"Foolish girl!" The guard glowered at her from the safety beneath the waves. "It's time I took you back to the palace."

"But—"

"No argument."

Under Ceilp's watchful eye, Muireen reluctantly turned her back on the bright glimmer of the world above. Her trick would not work a second time.

As they descended through the waters, the greeny-blue quality of the light seemed darker than before, the liquid murmur of the sea a poor echo of the dancing wind and calling gulls who owned the sky.

She closed her eyes, recalling the face and form of the human she'd seen. His cheeks were burnished bronze by the sun and wind, his dark hair worn short. He had seemed not much older than herself, and she wondered why he was all alone in a boat so far from shore.

"The storm's coming in," Ceilp said. "Feel it in the current? It's best we left the surface when we did,"

Muireen did feel it, the first tremor of turmoil and churn, and her heart squeezed in fear for the fisherman playing his music far above. He was some distance from land, and his craft was so small. But there was no use in begging to return to the surface.

Too late, anyhow—the pearly turrets of the palace rose ahead, glowing with luminescence as the water darkened.

At the entrance to her tower, Muireen pulled a long strand of pearls from her hair and turned to Ceilp.

"Thank you for your escort," she said, handing the guard the pearls. "I will always remember my first journey to the surface."

"It was an honor." Ceilp said. "I am glad no trouble came of it."

"Of course not, with such a capable guard as yourself." Muireen smiled. "I truly am grateful for your service today." Most of all, she was glad of seeing the mortal man. But small fishes had big mouths, and she dared not speak of that encounter. Nothing but trouble would follow if the king knew of it.

"Muireen!" her sister Aila called from the near tower. "You've returned safely! Come and tell us about your first breath of air."

Ceilp made Muireen a formal bow. "I will inform your father that your birthday journey is complete and you've returned safely. Good evening, princess."

"Fine swimming to you," Muireen replied.

As her her guard departed, she glanced up and up. Barely at the edge of her vision, a faint turbulence roiled. The storm.

Her heart clenched at the thought of the fisherman—but her sisters were expecting her. No matter how much she wanted to surge back to the surface, she could not.

At least, not yet.

※

Eiric ducked his head as another wave crashed against the side of the boat, the harsh spray coating his face and hands. The wind pummeled him, and he reefed the small sail close, trying to control his craft in the face of the raging elements.

Most of the afternoon he'd spent frustratingly becalmed. When he'd tired of playing his whistle he'd turned to mending the nets, though most of his supplies for such were back at his cottage. Still, it passed the time.

Finally, when the sun dipped low, racing its own reflection in the water, the breeze had sprung up. Brisk at first, then brisker still, until Eiric's boat ran before a fierce storm. No matter how nimbly he sailed, his heart clenched within him as the shadow of the clouds overtook the last pewter light shimmering on the sea.

All too soon, he'd been engulfed. Dark gray clouds matched the waves, and he lost all sight of the setting sun. Navigating by instinct, he prayed he was still headed east, and not out over the open waters, where death awaited with outstretched arms.

It took all his skill to keep his boat running upon the backs of the waves, and not directly into their hungry mouths. He did not always succeed. Fingers numb with cold, he fought the storm for what felt like hours. His ears were deafened by the rasp of the wind, his eyes stung nearly blind with salt.

Then he heard it—the crack and smash of waves breaking against stone.

He was near land, but not the sweet cove of the bay beside the village. No, he must have come in to the south where mighty cliffs rose, uncaring that a mortal life would be dashed to nothing against the rocks.

Aye, he'd wanted land. But not like this.

Forcing his hands steady, Eiric wove his boat through the water and wind, fighting to turn aside from the implacable cliffs. Hope strained his lungs as the sound of wave on stone began to fade.

Then he was pitched forward as the boat struck something in the water. Crying out, he grabbed for the side. Missed. A glimpse of black rock, splintered wood, and then the sea closed over his head, cold and relentless.

. . .

CHAPTER/scene

Muireen waited until indigo darkness filled the sea before slipping out of her tower room. The night guards were posted to keep watch for things coming into the palace, not sneaking out. Keeping to the shadows, she swam carefully until she was some distance from the pearly towers.

Then, with powerful sweeps of her tail, she drove herself up to the surface, angling for the place she'd seen the fisherman. The closer she rose to the ceiling of the sea, the more turbulent the water. The bottoms of the waves pulled at her hair and tried to unbalance her, the swirl of storm spinning her about.

Just before breaking into the air, she recalled her training, and prepared her lungs for the transition.

Harsh wind battered her face and shoulders, so much spray in the air that for a dizzying moment her body did not respond. She choked on salt, on the horrible emptiness above the waves. Shuddering, she thrashed her tail, lifting her high enough that her lungs finally responded.

Gasping, Muireen swept her sticky hair from her face and searched desperately for the fisherman's boat. How could he survive such a rage of smacking water and tearing wind?

There was no sign of him.

Surely he'd made for land at the first sign of storm, and was even now safely at home, far from the grasp of the sea. But even as the sensible part of herself argued that she ought to dive down to safety, something else pulled her on, toward the memory of where the island of Eire lay.

At length a strange sound came to her ears, a rhythmic crash and crack. Before she understood it, the storm threw her forward, and she smacked against the side of a rock jutting from the water.

Pain flashed through her, and she ducked down, away from the greedy hands of the weather above. The power of the storm was blunted beneath the water, and she drew in a steadying gulp, searching for calm. She should not be here, where the rocks waited to tear her body.

A bit of wood brushed her arm, borne by the sucking current. Then another.

It took a moment to realize what it meant.

The debris was new and sharp-edged. Some craft had hit the rocks and wrecked. Panic flashing through her, she turned in a circle, every sense alert.

There! Overhead, she saw the remains of a boat smashing up against the stone. And there...

Time slowed.

Muireen's blood beat stronger than the surge of the waves in her ears. She dove, hands outstretched, for the form of the man sinking to his death. It was the fisherman, and for an instant she saw a silver thread stretching from her heart to his, a path of starlight, of fate.

Then she reached him and wrapped her arms about him, pulling them both up, up, driving through the rough water until she reached the harsh air again. He was heavy against her, and cold, his head lolling. The waves beat at them like fists.

Desperately, she swam, steering away from the terrifying crash of sea on stone. Surely the land held more than the hungry rocks. Breath heaving, she scanned the shoreline. There! A bare crescent of sand beckoned, barely wide enough for a single body, framed by jagged black stone. She forced herself forward, her timing and agility slowed by the body in her arms. The tide threw her up against the side of a rock.

She twisted, and the stone left a long, painful scrape down her tail.

Then she was through the worst of the surf, and felt the land rise up, pulling away from the sea. Teeth bared, she thrashed forward, for the first time cursing her tail. Ungainly against the rough grains of sand, she pushed the fisherman before her until he was out of reach of the waves.

He was not breathing.

Awkwardly, she turned him on his side and thumped his back.

"Come now, human," she cried. "Spit out the sea and live. Please."

As if hearing her, his body convulsed. A gush of water emitted from his mouth and he shuddered. Muireen laid her hand between his shoulders and willed him to breathe.

Another shiver wracked him. He coughed again, and then she felt the blessed pull of air into his body.

"Yes," she sighed.

His dark hair hid his face and she carefully pushed the sodden strands aside so that she might see his features. His cheeks were pale, but regaining color even as she watched. His lips were too soft for the rest of his face—the sharp nose and stern forehead, the black slashes of his brows.

As she hovered over him, his eyes opened. They were a wild, stormy blue. Muireen stared into those depths, and felt the hook set deep inside her heart.

"You." His voice was a whispered croak. "Saved me."

"Shh," she said. "Rest."

He closed his eyes and lay his head back down on the sand, but still he breathed. Beneath her hand, Muireen could feel his heart beating. Her fisherman would live.

But she refused to leave him alone through the night.

As the water pulled and pushed in and out of the little cove, she held him close and sang him the songs of the sea people in her low, husky voice. The storm quieted, and as the sky cleared she was amazed to see a shimmer of tiny lights overhead—the luminescence of the night that mortals called stars.

After a time, she realized the blackness was fading, nibbled away at one side of the sky by the approaching dawn. She could not stay, could not risk discovery, though it tore her in two to leave her fisherman.

"Farewell," she whispered, bending to lay her lips against his.

Their breaths mingled, and a salty drop fell from her eye to splash against his cheek. He stirred, and in a sudden panic, Muireen thrashed herself back into the shelter of the sea. The water took her in, cool and welcoming, concealing the secret of her tail.

She hid behind one of the rocks that had battered her. Her body rocked up and down with the now-quiet waves as she peeked out and watched her fisherman lying upon the beach. Watched as he sat up and rubbed at his face, then looked about him like a man who had misplaced something important. Watched as he rose, and winced, and cast a regretful glance at the splintered boards that had washed ashore in the night.

Watched as he turned his back on the sea and trudged away from her into the light of dawn.

❀

Currents of cold water wrapped about Muireen as she swam into the dusky waters of the Sea Witch's domain.

She should not be there, venturing into the clammy kelp beds in pursuit of a vain hope, but for the past week she had been unable to think of anything except her fisherman. The sight of him walking away from her haunted her dreams, and her waking hours, until she could barely eat or carry on a conversation.

It will pass, Muireen told herself, but every day was worse than the one before. She could not help remembering the silver thread she'd glimpsed, tying them together. Was this the reason she could scarcely sleep?

A low moaning sound reached her ears, like the call of a whale, but full of menace, not melancholy. She shivered and swam on, toward a blot of darkness visible ahead.

The blackness resolved to a cave mouth. Muireen halted, her hair drifting about her. It was not too late to turn back.

Oh, but it was. The moment she'd glimpsed the fisherman, it had been too late.

With a steadying gulp, she dove forward, into the cave. It was even colder inside the black stone walls, and a faint greenish light emanated from the depths, a tunnel, leading her on. The sound grew louder, vibrating through Muireen's scales, until she could hardly think, let alone swim.

Then she emerged into a cavern, and the noise ceased. The green light illuminated pale fishes with bulbous eyes and a few sickly strands of waterweed growing from the cavern's sides.

But most of all, it showed the Sea Witch floating in the center of the space, her white eyes turned on Muireen. Hideous white eyes, white skin the color of dead things, suckered tentacles waving from her head, instead of hair. Where her tail should have been was only a swirl of blackness, as though a squid had ejected its ink and fled.

I should not have come. Muireen's chest tightened, and she turned to flee. Rough stone greeted her, slimed with the secretions of moon snails. The tunnel she'd traveled down was gone. Panic racing through her, she pivoted to face the witch.

"Sea King's daughter," the witch said, her voice carrying the memory of a thousand shipwrecks, "I am so very pleased to see you. Tell me, why have you come?"

For a fleeting moment, Muireen was tempted to say it was all a mistake. Tempted to plead that the Sea Witch release her, unharmed, that it had been nothing more than a foolish dare.

But her heart ached where fate bound her to her mortal man. There could be no simple escape from that snare.

"There is a fisherman," she said.

The witch opened her mouth and let out a keening cry of laughter. "Oh yes, yes. One of those. Delicious. Shall I tell you the terms of the bargain?"

"But you don't know what I want," Muireen protested.

The Sea Witch's blank eyes stared at her. "Of course I do. You want to take on the semblance of a mortal girl, so that you might seek out the fisherman you are so foolishly in love with."

"I'm not in love." Even as she spoke the words, though, a part of Muireen hummed in agreement. "How could I be in love with some ungainly human? I am a princess of the sea."

The witch held up a hand, black webs spread between her clawed fingers.

"I can see the strands of fate wrapped about your heart," she said. "You were wise to come to me, for I can give you what you desire. For a price."

"What is the price?" Muireen's lips felt numb, as though she'd swum through the poisoned strands of a jellyfish.

"You must give me your voice," the witch says. "In return, I will be able to transform you into human form—but only for a year and a day. At the end of that time, you will turn back into a mer and re-enter the sea forever."

A year and a day. It was not long enough—yet it was far better than nothing at all.

"I agr—"

"Wait." The Sea Witch smiled, showing rows of serrated teeth. "When you return to your form, you will come to me to reclaim your voice. And you will give me one more thing—the bitter tears of your desolation. For in such heart-wrenching sorrow lies great power."

Muireen glanced away from the witch's horrifying countenance and thought desperately, but she could see no alternative. Distasteful as the bargain might be, she must take it.

"It seems I have little choice," she said.

"That is truer than all the pearls in the sea," the witch said. "Now, open your mouth and sing your favorite lullaby."

From somewhere, she conjured a glass bottle and held it over her head.

"Sing," she commanded.

Muireen began, and she could almost see her voice disappearing into the bottle. Slowly, the glass turned a translucent silver-blue: the exact hue of her scales. When the song ended, she glanced down to see that her tail was leached to a sickly gray.

Her gasp of dismay was only a breath. When she tried to form words, nothing came out but little bursts of warm water.

"It is done." The witch tucked the bottle away. "Go now, daughter of the Sea King. Rise to the land, and when you exit the sea, your tail will disappear and you will walk upon two legs. Or attempt to." She let out a harsh cackle. "I will look forward to your visit a year and a day hence."

The Sea Witch raised her hands and pushed, and a sudden

dark current swept Muireen up. It bore her quickly through the tunnel and past the wavering kelp, through indigo waters to turquoise, and then pale blue.

With one final surge, it pushed her upon the shore—the same small beach where she'd taken her fisherman.

Muireen gasped and coughed, her lungs unprepared for the transition. Then fierce pain gripped her from the waist down. She opened her mouth, but had no voice to scream. She could only watch in mute horror as her tail disappeared, leaving two spindly stalks in its place.

Legs.

That she must learn to walk upon.

❧

For five days, Eiric rested in the bed he'd inherited from his parents. The white walls of the cottage wrapped around him, the breeze rustled the thatch overhead, reassuring him that he was safe.

The villagers brought him broth and helped him rise to use the chamber pot. Biddy was there more often than most, but Eiric did not have the energy to turn away. Fevers wrung him, and a thousand aches from being tumbled against the rocks below the cliffs.

"It's a miracle he survived," the people whispered. "He is truly blessed by the gods."

He did not feel blessed, but cursed. Whenever he closed his eyes to rest, which was often, nightmares of the crashing sea sucked him under.

Again and again he fought to turn his boat, heard the sickening crack of the hull on stone, felt the hungry cold grasp of the waves. The only thing that made his dreams bearable was the memory of a young woman's face, looking down at him.

Her eyes were the warm blue of the sea at midday. Her long hair held brightness and shadow, tangled with sea foam. Her skin was pale, her hands upon his brow cool and welcome.

Each time he woke, Eiric was filled with a pang of loss. Had he imagined her, or had she rescued him from the storm's hunger?

A smaller, more urgent loss pained him as well, and that was the loss of his boat. He would have to go back to using the small leather coracle that had been his first vessel. No more venturing out into the deep deep waters, where the catch was best. No more room to stow his finest nets. He feared it would be a lean winter.

Biddy would feed you, his thoughts offered up.

He could not think of it—not when the pearl-skinned girl haunted his dreams. And his wakings.

A week unspooled past, and Eiric finally woke feeling... not rested, exactly, but well enough to get out of bed and see if anything salvageable had washed ashore in the tiny cove that had saved him.

He took a hunk of bread stuffed with cheese, a skin of water, and a stout walking stick that had belonged to his Da, and set out over the headland. The sun warmed his shoulders and the top of his head, and he felt as though his life might be worth living, after all.

It took him some time to reach the narrow path cutting through the bracken that led to the tiny beach. He'd had to rest often, and twice refilled his water skin from the small stream that crisscrossed his path.

His lunch called to him, but he'd be better off saving it for after he'd visited the shore. A reward for the hike back up the steep trail, which, in truth, he was not looking forward to.

For now, though, gravity aided him and soon the crash of the waves against the cliffs filled the air. It took all his concentration to keep his feet under him as he made the last descent to the sliver of sand below.

His boots hit the sand and he stood a moment catching his balance and his breath. Then lost them both when he saw he was not alone.

She was there—the maiden who haunted his thoughts, sitting huddled against a rock, facing the sea. Her long hair covered her like a cloak, but she was naked, the pearly skin of her limbs shining in the sun.

Heartbeat thundering in his ears, Eiric glanced about the little cove, looking for her clothing, or her selkie skin, anything that would help him learn what kind of creature she was. For though she appeared mortal, he knew deep in his soul that she was a magical being.

Sensing his presence, she spun awkwardly about and fixed him with her blue, blue eyes.

"Don't be afraid," he said, his voice a hoarse whisper. "I won't harm you, I swear it."

He could not bear it if she fled back into the waves.

To his relief, she gave him a tentative smile and made no move toward the shining water.

"I'm Eiric," he said, little caring that he might be giving his name to a faerie. Even if she were a fey maiden, he feared he'd already lost his heart to her. Anything more was a trifle. "Do you understand me?"

She nodded, and the beauty in her face made him weak at the knees.

"Have you a name you go by?" he asked.

Again she nodded. Then, with a stricken look, she brought her hand up to her throat and shook her head.

"You cannot speak?"

She opened her mouth, but no sound came out.

"Well then." Eiric settled on the sand. "Still, you and I might converse together in other ways."

A quick nod of her head.

"Where have you come from?"

She turned, hair slipping off one pale shoulder, and gestured at the sea. So, it was as he thought.

"Might I call you Muireann? It means 'sea fair' in my language. And you are very fair."

She blushed slightly and dropped her gaze to the sand. Eiric was hard pressed not to stare openly at her nakedness. Instead, he pulled off his shirt and handed it to her.

"You might put this on, if you like."

Giving him a smile as quick as a silver fish, she held the garment up, studying it a moment before pulling it over her head. She had difficulty with the arm holes, and he reached to help her, drawing one fine-boned hand through the sleeve, and then the other.

"You're not used to clothing, I take it."

He was rewarded with another of her darting smiles.

"I think..." He stared at the waves gnashing upon the rocks. "I think you saved me, sea-fair maiden. Was that you?"

In answer, she rose to her knees a bit unsteadily, then cupped his face between her hands. He held very still, as though she were a wild thing he did not want to frighten. Gods, but she was beautiful. And strong, and brave, by all indications.

Softly, she kissed him on the forehead.

Her touch was enough to undo him. Eiric gathered her into

his arms and held her close. Her heart beat fast, and her skin was cool, but not cold.

Gently, quietly, they kissed, and his heart, at last, felt as though it had come home.

⚜

Muireen could scarce believe her luck. Her fisherman had come to seek her out! Joy surged through her in great waves, despite the awkward feel of her new body. And though she could not speak, they understood one another well enough.

She sat, nestled against his side, and marveled at the warmth of his human body. Together, they watched the waves come in, until the tide nibbled at their toes. With a sigh, Eiric turned to look at her.

"The sun's soon to be setting. I suppose you must return to the sea now, fair maid, though my heart weeps at losing you."

She shook her head at him.

"No?" His eyes widened. "Is it possible you might come live with me, and be my bride?"

She hesitated, but there was no way to explain that she must return to the sea in a year's time. That was a dim cloud on the horizon. After all, a year was a very long while.

She answered him with a kiss.

"Then, my love, we'd best away before dark. We can come another time to search for the wreckage of my boat—if any still remains."

She nodded, and let him pull her to her feet. For a moment she tottered, but with his help found her balance. Walking was more difficult, though, and she let out a little hiss of pain when she stubbed her toe on an outcropping.

"Sit here a moment." He guided her to a rock, then bent and took off his foot coverings.

They came in two parts, she was interested to observe. Mortal clothing was very strange.

"I fear my boots will be too large, and trip you further in any case. But my socks will give you some protection."

He held out the cloth wrappings, then helped her don them. They were warm from his body, and smelled rather strongly, but she was glad of the layer between her tender new skin and the ground.

"Now, Muireann, we must climb to the top of the headland and walk a fair bit before reaching my village. Luckily, it will be dark, so we can avoid the worst of the questions until tomorrow. Are you ready?"

She nodded. No matter what difficulties lay ahead, and she was certain there would be many, it would be worth it with her fisherman by her side.

꧁❧꧂

A moon passed, and though the villagers still treated Muireen with suspicion, they had come to accept she was there to stay. All except the flame-haired Biddy, who spat and made the sign of protection whenever their paths crossed.

Together, Muireen and Eiric had managed to pull his wrecked boat from the rocks. Paired with another ruined craft, they'd cobbled together an ugly but seaworthy boat that could take the two of them over the waves.

For though Eiric tried to protest, Muireen was determined to go out with him upon the sea. She'd let him fish alone in his small coracle, and helped him gut and salt the fish he returned with, but she refused to waste their precious time by pining on land, waiting for him.

It was an advantage of not being able to speak, that she simply demonstrated her intent with actions. Though he pleaded, Muireen refused to leave her place at the prow of the boat, and so they set out together.

They worked well together, plying the nets and taking in the fish, And if once or twice Muireen spotted the trailing hair of a mer warrior beneath their boat, she was not alarmed.

No doubt her father had been full of wrath when he'd discovered her bargain with the Sea Witch—but such things could not be broken. Instead, it seemed he'd sent his guard to keep watch on her.

In the evenings, Eiric played his whistle as they sat before the fire in their little cottage. Muireen learned how to cook, though she was ever wary of the flames. She learned to sew, and to knit ungainly socks and sweaters that, while not lovely to behold, kept them warm as the night darkened.

After two moons, she was with child.

"Please jump the broom with me," Eiric said. "We should be handfasted. If not for your sake, then for the babe."

Muireen had refused each time he'd spoken of it before. She was far more comfortable going from cottage to sea and back, content in the simple life they'd woven for themselves. Putting herself on display before the villagers made the old fear rise, that they'd see her as a mer creature and kill her on the spot.

But for him, and the little creature now swimming in her belly, she agreed.

The day of the ceremony dawned bright and clear. Eiric and Muireen broke their fast, and then he turned to her, smiling.

"My love, I'll leave you now to make ready. Orla has kindly agreed to come help you prepare."

They kissed, and then a knock came at the cottage door. Shy, dark-haired Orla stepped in, carrying a dress the color of sea foam at sunrise.

"I brought you this. It's been in my family for two generations. I thought I might be wed in it, but..." She glanced at Eiric, regret in her eyes. "Anyhow, I'd like you to wear it, Muireann."

Muireen brought her hands together and bowed in thanks. It was very generous. Perhaps—the thought stabbed her heart—perhaps in ten months, when she was gone, Orla might take her place.

Or perhaps not. The love between herself and Eiric was a strong, true bond. She feared he might go mad from losing her, which was part of why she'd refused to wed him. But now there was the babe.

Smiling, she set her hand over her belly. At least there would be some part of her remaining when she returned to the sea.

The ceremony was held on the headland, the bright ocean shining beneath. Eiric said the words, and Muireen emphatically nodded her agreement. Together they let the priestess tie a braided cord about their clasped hands, then jumped the broom while the villagers cheered.

That night they feasted on mutton and ale, and Muireen felt, for a small time, part of the human world.

Despite her insistence on going out in the boat with him, the time came when Muireen's belly was too large for her to be of much use. Too, a melancholy had settled in her soul. Only three months remained until she must leave Eiric forever and return to the sea. Ah, and the Sea Witch would reap well her harvest of tears, for already the sorrow of parting felt unbearable.

Eiric attributed her moods to the state of her body, and was ever patient and kind with her. If he feared that the babe growing within her was less than human, he never spoke a word.

She worried, though, with thoughts that kept her awake and fretting into the cold nights. What if the child was born with fins, or a tail? What if she and the baby were cast out, or killed?

Be well, she thought fiercely at the little life inside her. *Be human.*

From one day to the next, spring came upon the land. The days grew longer and a warm wind blew over the sea.

And Muireen bore a baby girl, with no fins or tail, and her father's dark hair.

"We shall call her Brea," her father said, holding her up and smiling bright as the dawn.

Caught between great joy and great sorrow, Muireen smiled at him through her tears, and nodded. Now that her baby, her daughter, was born, she knew the pain of leaving would be doubled.

But for the month that remained to her upon the land, she could not let that shadow fall over her days. So, with great effort, she pushed it away. Instead, she concentrated on all the perfect moments: Eiric's smile and the scent of him, the soft skin of her daughter, the warmth the three of them made, curled up together in their bed.

The moon waned, and went dark, and that night Muireen dreamed of the Sea Witch.

"Tomorrow," the witch said. "Tomorrow you come back to the sea. If you are not in the water's embrace by sunset, your legs will disappear and you will be revealed for what you truly are. And you will be killed for it."

Muireen woke, shivering, and knew the witch spoke truly. Even if Eiric tried to protect her, he would not be able to stand against the villagers. In her mer form she would be too strange, too frightening. They would take her life, and little Brea's as well.

When Eiric woke and made ready to go out to his boat, she caught his arm and shook her head at him. *Don't go.*

"What's this, love?" He gazed down tenderly at her.

She touched her heart, then his, then glanced down at the babe sleeping in her arms. This was their last day together.

"Aye, I love you and our family with all my heart. But I must go out and fish."

She took his arm again, all her sorrow rising in her eyes, and he relented.

"Very well. But only for today."

She gave a small nod. Yes. Only that day—for tomorrow she would be gone forever.

She packed a lunch, put Brea in her sling, and they roved out over the headland. Eiric collected a bouquet of wildflowers for her, and she kissed him, wishing that she could speak of what was to come.

They ate, drank cool water from the stream, and she led him to the path down to the tiny beach where they'd first met. The first shadows from the lowering sun began to fall across the land.

"Should we not be returning home?" he asked.

She shook her head and started down the path. How comfortable her legs had become in a year, how deftly she stepped around stones, feeling herself balance upright in the air. Even carrying the small weight of her baby, it seemed a simple thing, to stride across the land.

When they reached the sliver of sand, she sat, facing the ocean.

Eiric settled beside her, one strong arm around her shoulders as she fed Brea for the last time. When the baby was finished, Muireen handed her to her father, her arms aching with loss.

The banners of the clouds were beginning to turn silvery orange. Heart aching, Muireen stood and stripped off her clothing: shawl, blouse, skirts and shoes. She unbraided her hair until it fell loose about her shoulders, brushing her back and belly.

Eiric watched, his gaze solemn.

When she went to her knees before him, a single tear slipped from his eye.

"Ah, beloved." His voice was choked with sorrow. "Is this our end, then? Must you return to the sea and leave me cruelly alone?"

She set her hand on Brea's head, then looked deep into the eyes of her fisherman. *Be strong, for our daughter*, she thought, even as her heart was breaking.

Their lips met. The sun dipped lower, kissing the horizon.

Then Muireen pulled away and flung herself back, into the arms of the sea. Pain ripped through her as her legs cleaved together. She gasped, and in that moment found her voice.

"Remember me, Eiric," she called. "You are my true love."

"As you are mine, sea maid." He rose, cradling their child in his arms. "Will I ever see you again?"

"Look for me in the bright dance of the waves. In the foam upon the shore. Where you go, there, too, my heart goes."

Uncaring of the pain—what was one more stab when her soul was shattering?—she hooked her fingers beneath one of the scales of her newfound tail and ripped it free. Even as a dark current swirled in to bear her away to the Sea Witch, she flung the scale to shore.

The last thing she heard was the sobbing of her husband, the thin wail of their child.

❁

"Oh, such bounty," crooned the Sea Witch as she captured Muireen's tears. "Not only mourning the loss of your love but of your baby. Such power."

At last Muireen pulled away from the witch, shuddering, her grief drained dry.

"A pity that's the last of it." The Sea Witch held up the vial containing Muireen's sorrow. "Or is it? Tell me—where is your missing scale?" She pointed at the gap in Muireen's tail.

"I threw it to him," Muireen said, defiantly.

"Ahh. Listen then, and I will offer you joy and despair in equal measure. Every year, upon this anniversary, I can use my magic to let you see the world of the mortals, via the scale you left behind. I hope your husband keeps it safe and close by."

"He will."

"Then you will be able to gaze upon him, and your child, for a brief time And when you say farewell and once again the anguish falls upon you, I will take it for my own uses. Do you agree?"

"Will he be able to see me, too?"

"Of course, for that will make the pain all the greater." The witch gave her a horrible smile. "Since your pain prolongs my life, I welcome it."

Muireen did not like to think she was helping the Sea Witch in any way. And yet, to be able to see Eiric and her daughter once a year, however briefly, was a chance she could not refuse.

"Very well."

"Good! And luckily you'll be out of the palace dungeons next year, just in time. Now go, back to your foolish father and worthless siblings, and give them my regards."

Again the dark current bore Muireen through the reaches of the sea, depositing her where the indigo water faded into greeny blue. Tiredly, she swam toward the pearly towers of the palace, ready to bear whatever punishment her father thought just.

Some day, though, she vowed she would make the Sea Witch reunite her and her mortal love.

❦

The first time the silver scale lit with Muireen's image, Eiric thought he was dreaming. Gods knew, he dreamt of her constantly. But to his surprise, he could hear her, too.

"I have not much time, love," she said. "It is only through the magic of the Sea Witch that I may look upon you. Tell me, how do you fare? And our child?"

He showed her Brea, sleeping in her crib, told her all was well. Too soon, the light of the scale began to dim.

"When shall I see you again?" he cried.

"Next year." Her voice faded, and the cool silvery blue scale reflected back the light of his candle.

Ah, the pain was worse after seeing her face. And yet, knowing that she still lived, that she cared for him and their child, was enough to soothe the worst of the ache.

Every year, for a brief time, magic imbued the scale and Eiric was able to tell Muireann he loved her still. For he did, the flame of that love still burning fresh within him. He showed her how their daughter grew, and shared her milestones—first steps, first words, first swim in the sea which, thankfully, had not resulted in her sprouting fins or a tail.

"She is not a mer," Muireann said, "for never have our kind bred true with humans."

"I'm not certain she's entirely human, though," Eiric replied. "There is an odd touch of magic about her."

"Then perhaps she's a fey water creature of some kind. But she must find her own destiny."

Then the scale went quiet, and all other words must wait for another year.

It was not a pleasant thing, to bide so long, but it was enough. Eiric replayed their brief conversations in his head, traced her beloved features in memory, over and over. Their daughter grew into a lonely, quiet girl, and his heart ached within him for her solitude. He never spoke of her mother. That burden he would bear alone.

Many years passed, until one day while Eiric was out on his boat, the sky darkened with a sudden storm. He'd weathered storms aplenty but this one felt different—full of menace. He quickly stowed his nets, the memory of the fierce gale that had nearly taken his life shivering through him.

This storm tasted the same, the air heavy and metallic with the rising wind.

Then it was upon him, waves churning, spray blinding his

eyes. This time, he was too far from land, fishing over the deep waters. There would be no escape from the ocean's wrath.

Still, he tried, fighting to keep his boat upon the waves and not under them, bailing when he could. Although Brea was nearly grown, he did not want to leave her an orphan, both parents lost to the sea.

But he was given no choice in the matter. A great, black wave rose over his boat, then smashed down, punching him to the depths.

Eiric floated, blinking against the salt water burning his eyes. Here, beneath the waves, it was strangely peaceful. The last of his breath left his body in a silver strand of bubbles, racing away toward the roiling surface. He let them go.

Then Muireann was there, floating before him. She pressed a bottle to his lips and he drank, then gagged on the foul secretion.

"Swallow it," she said, tears in her voice. "I cannot you save you, otherwise."

Coldness all about him, Eiric swallowed. Then screamed as the cold burned away. Something terrible was happening to him, yet his sea maiden held him close.

Finally, shuddering, the pain passed. He looked up at his beloved.

"Are we dead?" he asked, amazed to find he could form the words.

"No, my love." She smiled at him. "You are no longer human, however. There is no return to the surface for you."

"As long as I might remain here, beneath the sea with you, I care not. Wherever you go—"

"There my heart also goes," she finished the words for him.

Together, webbed hands clasped, they swam, tails flashing through the water. Away from the storm and darkness, away from the cold, to an enchanted palace in the far south, made of shining coral.

There they rule to this day, wearing crowns of pearl and mantles of kelp, the Sea Queen and her once-mortal love.

Author's Note: The story first appeared in Once Upon A Kiss, an anthology of romantic faerietale retellings. *The Little Mermaid* was my inspiration for this story. And while I wanted to incorporate some of the tragic elements from Hans Christian Andersen's original tale, I still wanted a fairytale happy ending for Muireen and her fisherman, no matter the sorrow it took them to get there.

BREA'S TALE

CHAPTER 1
WATERBORNE

CONNACHT, Eire, 9ᵗʰ century

Brea Cairgead bent over her father's second-best fishing net, her fingers crusted with salt as she mended the coarse weave. A warm wind blew in from the sea, ruffling her long, dark hair and the thatched roofs of the cottages, and making her neighbor's bright flowers sway.

The sky overhead was a pale summer blue, the weather fair for a good catch. Heat reflected from the whitewashed wall behind Brea, and before her lay the harbor and an endless view of the broad back of the sea.

Brea glanced at the waters, searching for a sign of her father's boat, but there was nothing to see but the white tips of the waves. He would not return home until deep into the twilight hours.

"The long days cannot be wasted," he'd told her once, when she had complained of his absence. "Come winter there will be time enough to sit by the fire and tell tales—but if I do not work now, what will we have to eat when the darkness descends?"

And so Brea had learned to bite her tongue and accept loneliness as her constant companion. The other children had always treated her warily, and as they grew into young men and women, paired off. No one came courting for Brea.

Finally, two summers ago, she had discovered why.

Brea shook her head, trying to dispel her melancholy mood. Sometimes she thought she should visit the sacred spring, located some distance from the village, and fasten a fluttering thread of a wish upon the hawthorn tree growing there—but she had no wishes to leave for the Fair Folk. All her hopes were kept imprisoned deep in her heart. Speaking them aloud, even tying a wish upon the tree's branches, would only increase her sorrow sevenfold.

I wish for a true love of my own. I wish I had sisters and brothers. And the biggest, most painful of them all: *I wish I could remember my mother.*

Her father would not speak of Brea's mother. If Brea pressed him too closely, he would storm out of the small cottage and down the road to Biddy's Pub, and not return until he was reeling drunk, the fumes of *uisce beatha* filling the room until Brea barely could draw breath.

So, she had stopped asking.

But two years ago, on a summer afternoon much like this one, something had possessed her to go over to her father's bed and pull the mattress up. It was heavy, stuffed with straw and a thin top layer of goose feathers. She'd grunted as she heaved it up, bracing it against her shoulder.

And found, lying against the thin slats of the bed frame, something altogether mysterious.

It shimmered, opalescent, roughly the size of her hand.

Brea snatched it up and let the mattress fall back onto the frame, then went to the window to examine her find.

She might have thought it was a fish scale, but no fish she had ever seen would have a scale so large. It was flat and thin and roughly triangular. She held it up to her nose and sniffed, but it carried no odor. A quick taste yielded a faint salt flavor, but that might have been the sweat from her own hands.

Brea turned the scale back and forth in the light, so caught up in its rainbow shimmer that she did not see her father arrive. One moment she was admiring the scale's glimmer, the next it was yanked from her hand. She looked up in surprise to see a storm gathering in her father's eyes.

"Da," she said, hoping for an answer before the squall broke. "What is it?"

"Something best left alone," he said.

He stalked to the bed, paused a moment, then thrust the scale beneath his mattress once more. Brea caught the tender flash in his eyes, like the flicker of the winter lights that streamed across the sky, if one looked for them.

"Does it have to do with my mother?" she asked.

His expression shuttered then.

"I'll be at Biddy's," he said, turning on his heel.

That time, he had not come home for two days. Brea did not broach the topic of the scale with him again, and when she next went looking for it, the mysterious object was nowhere to be found.

She was a clever girl, though, and slowly a sketch of the past unfolded itself. Her mother had come from the sea—some sort of ocean being who had become, for a time, a wife. Surely she was not a selkie, for then Brea would have discovered a sealskin. Or transformed herself into a sleekly furred sea creature.

The more she thought on it, the more convinced she grew that her mother had not been a normal human woman, but a mystery born of water and starlight.

It would explain so much.

From a young age, Brea had been nearly as comfortable in the water as she was on land. At first, she had thought the other children disliked her because of her uncanny swimming ability—but it was more than that. It was the fey blood that ran in her veins. No wonder the other villagers treated her with distance.

I'm still just myself! she wanted to cry out. *Just a girl.* Other than her talent in the water, there was nothing remarkable about her.

Indeed, since the discovery of the scale, and the notion that her mother had not been human, Brea had tried to reach something within herself. Something powerful and elusive and mysterious. If the neighbors looked askance at her, and no young men came to call, then she wanted to at least be able to do *something* otherworldly.

She'd taken to swimming alone in the cove a mile to the north. It was secluded and peaceful, with only the cries of the gulls to interrupt her efforts. But no matter what she did—held her breath underwater until she was dizzy or swam so far out into the waves that the shore was merely a blur—she never transformed into something more. Never found a wellspring of magic within her soul.

Her tears of frustration mingled with the seawater, and she beat at the waves with her fists. But still she did not change.

So that summer passed, and the next, and Brea found herself, at nearly seventeen turnings of the sun, with no clear future ahead.

Most of the girls of the village were courting or married.

Some had moved away to other towns, and the handful left single seemed content to care for aged parents or tend the crofts.

But that afternoon, mending the nets, Brea's soul stirred with a fierce longing for *more*.

A pity she had no bardic talent that would take her away to the halls of Tara. No wise ways with herbs and tonics or deft hand at healing.

Perhaps she might go to one of the large towns in the east, where no one knew her name or face. But even there, she would have no prospects. Who would hire a girl from a fishing village for more than a lowly serving wench—or worse?

Fingers re-plaiting the coarse rope, Brea stared sightlessly over the sea. The echo of the surf on the black rocks below was the beat of her heart, the sough of her sighs.

At length, when the shadows cooled and the sun began its long slide toward twilight, she set the nets aside and went in to make supper. Brown bread and fish stew with a few bartered vegetables. It was not much, but 'twas warm and would keep their bellies filled.

Dusk sifted over the village, the sea turning silver with the last light of day. Brea lit the beeswax candle on their plank tabletop, and the one in the window that stood sentinel for her father's return.

Worry did not start nibbling at her until most of the village quieted. Often her father returned late from hauling in his day's catch. He had no sons to help him, and as much as Brea begged, he sternly refused to take her out in his curricle.

Now, she wondered if he feared losing her to the deeps. Not by drowning, but perhaps from the heritage of her mother's blood rising up to claim her.

She went to the threshold and stood, looking down the

darkened and winding streets, hoping for a sight of her father's lantern. She waited a long time, until the lash of the rising wind and the spatter of stinging rain from the west drove her back inside. Black clouds scudded across the pewter sky, stealing the last light and extinguishing the stars.

Fear settled like a fist in her stomach.

The storm was blowing in off the ocean—where her father in his small boat was ever at the mercy of the winds.

For three days the tempest raged, tearing thatch from the roofs and carrying away anything left unattended. On the second day, the wind snatched their bucket straight off the hook outside the door. Brea had no hope of catching it. She watched helplessly from the window as the much-mended bucket rolled and clattered away down the street to smash against the sea wall.

She kept the hearth stoked with peat, and carefully portioned out the rest of the stew and bread, though it was tasteless in her mouth.

Da will return. She clutched the thought like a blanket, even as dark knowledge spread through her. He was likely never coming back.

On the morning of the fourth day, the dawn broke clear and golden. Brea grabbed her woolen shawl and hurried down to the dock.

She was not the first there. The gathered fishermen stood about the wreckage of a small boat, and Brea's steps slowed.

Please, no.

It was the remains of her father's curricle, flung ashore in the heart of the storm.

"Terrible sorry, lass," one of the men said, and the rest nodded, sympathy sitting uncomfortably on their worn faces.

"Likely won't be a body," another said.

The rest murmured in agreement.

Brea caught her breath on a sob and ran back to the cottage, tears blurring her vision so that she nearly lost her footing on the cobbles. She slammed the door behind her with a heavy thud, then sank to the floor, sobbing, as her heart broke thrice over.

The neighbors brought food and awkward comfort, but as the days passed their eyes hardened. After a week, old Biddy herself came to pay a visit.

"He's not coming back," she said. "'Tis a hard truth, but it must be faced."

Brea nodded. She could not yet speak the words aloud, but she knew in her heart that her father was gone. Taken by the sea.

Late at night, when sleep taunted her from the corners but would not settle upon her, Brea imagined her father and mother finally reunited. They sat together on thrones of coral, their hair lifted above their heads by the caress of the waters surrounding them, sunshine slanting down through the green sea in shafts of light to illuminate their pearly crowns.

It was a pretty thought, but in the light of day it burst like soap bubbles too-long exposed to the harsh air.

"What will you do now?" Biddy asked.

It was the question Brea had been pondering for days, and she was no closer to an answer. Her aunt in Corcaigh was half the length of the country away. Brea had never met the woman, as her aunt had left the fishing village as soon as she could and never looked back.

Biddy took Brea's silence for the lack of plan that it was.

"Well, now," the older woman said, her seamed face losing some of its sympathy. "Have you had any young man come courting?"

Of course not, and everyone in the village knew it.

"No," Brea said. She wove her fingers tightly together.

"Anyone who might take you in?"

"Can I not simply stay here on my own?" Brea asked, panic beginning to rise in her chest.

"No, lass. There's others have need of a fine, stout cottage to raise their families in. Why, the Reedys have seven people all beneath one roof. Their son and his new wife have a baby on the way."

"I could stay on and help them…"

Brea trailed off at the look in Biddy's eyes. The strange lass had been tolerated while her father was alive, but now there was no place for her in the village. A strained silence filled the room, chilly despite the peat burning upon the hearth.

"Very well," Brea said at last, dropping her gaze. "I'll gather my things and leave tomorrow."

What else could she do? Better to depart on her own, dignity intact, than have the villagers come and pitch her out of the cottage.

"There's a good girl." Biddy patted her knee. "I've a bit of coin set by I can give you for traveling money, and the roads should be safe enough."

Brea hoped so. Earlier in the year, reports had come of brigands prowling the countryside, but they seemed to have departed for richer pickings.

Where will I go? The question quivered on Brea's tongue, but she would get no answers from Biddy. Already the woman was taking her leave.

"I'll bring you the coin tomorrow morning," Biddy said, pausing at the threshold. "Nothing like an early start."

Brea nodded mutely. The sound of the door closing behind

Biddy echoed hollowly through the room. Through Brea's heart.

There was nothing for it except to pack up her meager belongings. In the morning, she took the good blanket from her father's bed and fashioned a bundle to hold her spare clothing, the kitchen knife and a wooden bowl, a linen kerchief, and the small carving of a fish her father had made one summer from a pearly shell.

She made one last effort to find the scale, and at last discovered it tucked behind the chimney. It was dark and opaque, all the light gone from it. She did not know if her father's death had made it so, or if it had become singed black from the heat of the fire. Regardless, she tucked it into the folds of her second-best skirt. It was all she had left of her parents.

Just after first light, Biddy rapped on the door. She nodded when she saw the bundle on the floor.

"Affix it to the end of a stout stick and carry it over your shoulder," she advised. "'Twill be easier to manage than carting it about in your arms."

"I will," Brea said, accepting the small purse the other woman held out. "Thank you for the coins."

"Hide them, and use them sparingly. Safe travels to you, Brea Cairgead."

It was a clear dismissal. Under Biddy's watchful eye, Brea tucked the purse away beneath her petticoat, then lifted the woolen blanket containing all her earthly possessions. Head high, despite the weight of stone in her heart, she stepped over the threshold and did not look back.

Down the street, she could see the Reedy daughter and her husband pulling a cart filled with household items. The air in the cottage would not even have time to cool before the new occupants took up residence.

"Farewell," Brea said.

To Biddy, to the huddle of cottages, to the rocky shore where she had last seen her father. There was no one and nothing else to say goodbye to. Taking a deep breath, Brea set her feet on the path leading southeast from Ardglass. The crying of gulls overhead gave voice to the tears she could not shed. The sigh of the surf was her own sorrow at leaving the only home she had ever known.

The path curved, and Brea knew that if she cared to turn and look, the village would no longer be visible. She did not turn, only set one foot on the earth, then the other. The bundle grew heavy in her arms, the wool prickling her palms.

Another league ahead lay a hazel wood. Perhaps she might find a stick there to attach her bundle to. And just before the wood was the sacred spring. She would tear a strip off her kerchief and tie it to the wishing tree there, hoping the Fair Folk would bestow luck upon her. Certainly, if anyone had need of it, 'twas herself.

The morning sun grew in strength, though the high clouds meant rain later. She hoped she would find shelter by the afternoon, or she would add being damp and cold to her overall misery.

But first the sacred spring, and the wood.

The path turned again, this time to follow the bright stream that led to the spring. The water made a merry sound, sunlight glinting off the surface, and Brea could not help but be a little cheered. She allowed herself to rest beside a tumbled granite boulder, and drank from her cupped hands. It was too much trouble to fetch the bowl from her bundle.

The stop revived her, and her bundle felt a bit lighter when she picked it up in her arms again. She was thankful for the burbling companionship of the stream as she strode up the heather-banked path.

At length the heart of the spring came in sight, just when Brea's shoulders were beginning to ache. She hurried the last few paces and set the blanket down on the ferny moss surrounding the spring. The wind rustled the leaves of the wood beyond, mimicking the sound of the sea.

Beside the cool, clear pool a bent hawthorn tree grew. Bright bits of cloth fluttered from its branches—wishes for luck and healing and to honor the Fair Folk who dwelt in the land.

Brea pulled her linen kerchief from the bundle and tore off a small strip. Luck she needed, surely, and a wish for safe travels as she went, friendless and alone, into the wide world. She knelt at the edge of the spring, dampness seeping through her skirts. Dipping her cupped hand into the water, she murmured a blessing upon the spirits of the place.

The water moistened her lips, but she was not fool enough to guzzle from the pool. She had a skin of water from Ardglass's stream to quench the thirst of the road. A soft wind shivered the surface of the water, and for a moment she thought she saw a face looking at her, a reflection of a fey woman with tangled greenish hair and stars for eyes.

Then a raven called harshly overhead, and the moment was broken.

Brea stood and made a curtsy to the waters. Her skirt was muddy at the knees.

"I hope I've not offended you," she said. "My apologies if I have. I'm but a wandering girl, and mean no harm."

The raven called again, a softer sound this time, as if reassuring Brea all was well. Heartened, she strode to the wishing tree and tied her strip of cloth to an empty branch. The cloths fluttered, some faded nearly white, others still bright with woad and berry juice.

A third time the raven called, taking startled flight into the air, and Brea heard the heavy tread of footsteps.

A moment later, three men crested the hill, their clothing rough, their beards unkempt. She shrank back, but there was nowhere to hide. She snatched up her bundle and backed toward the woods.

"A lass!" the black-haired one cried, looking at her as a wolf regards a lamb. "Aye, and it's a fair day for us indeed."

Greatly misliking his tone and the leers of his companions, she turned and ran for the trees.

But she was too slow, and awkwardly burdened. In four paces the men caught her, the first one grabbing her arm while the second snatched the bundle from her.

"A prize carrying a prize," the black-haired man said. "What's in the blanket, love?"

"Nothing of use to you," Brea said, her mind whirling as a dark fog of fear crept over her.

"We'll be the judge of that." The brigand holding the bundle pulled it open, letting the contents spill upon the ground.

The third man snatched up her bowl and knife, and toed her extra garments aside.

"Not much here," he said. "She's a right poor one."

"Shake out her clothing," the black-haired man said. "What's on the ground first, then what she's wearing."

He gave her a nasty smile.

Brea tried to pull away, but her captor's grasp was hard upon her. There was little chance she would escape the men until they were done with her. She swallowed hard, fearing what the next minutes would bring.

When the brigand took up her extra skirt, the blackened scale slipped free. It slid into the sacred pool with scarcely a ripple.

"What was that?" the second man asked, leaning over to peer into the water.

"Well?" Her captor shook her. "Answer."

"A scale I found on the beach," she said, her voice trembling. "I thought I might use it for a mirror, but it turned black."

"Not black now," the second man said. "Bright silver, it is."

"Well, fish it out," the black-haired leader demanded.

He marched Brea up to the pool's edge, where they could both see the scale, shining against the soft mud at the bottom.

The second man rolled up his dingy sleeves and sprawled on the moss. It was a desecration for him to reach his grimy hands into the clear waters, and Brea winced as he splashed about.

"I can't quite reach it," he said.

"Carrig, take his legs," the leader said, gesturing to the third man.

With much grunting and groaning, the second man was levered out over the surface of the pool.

"Still can't," he said.

"Then best hold your breath," the black-haired man said. "For I've a mind to fling you into this bedamned spring."

Brea bit back her cry of protest at the thought of a brigand's grimy body befouling those sacred waters. With the men's attention on the elusive scale, her captor's grip had loosened. If the moment presented itself, she would wrench herself free.

But then what? They had already proven they could catch her.

If she could gain the wood, perhaps she could lose them amidst the trees, or climb high enough that they could not pursue her.

Too many perilous chances to lose her life—yet she must act, and soon. She had no taste for becoming a brigand's doxy. Better to fall from a high branch and break her neck than the fate the men intended for her.

"I'll have to go under," the second man said. "Hold fast to me legs, Carrig."

He took a deep breath, then plunged his head and shoulders into the pool. In the clear water, Brea could see his hands flailing about, stirring up the soft silt at the bottom. The silver scale seemed to elude his grasp.

"Argh!" He surfaced with a shout and splash, red-faced.

"Try again," the black haired leader said.

"But—"

"'Tis your fault the bauble fell into the spring. Now fetch it out."

Hair plastered to his knobby head, the second man glared at his leader, but did not seem inclined to argue further. He blew two breaths out of his nostrils, then sucked in a mouthful of air and submerged his head and chest once more.

The bottom of the spring was murky now, but Brea glimpsed flashes of bright silver. And something else, lurking in the watery shadows beneath the bank. Something with green hair like kelp and glowing eyes, and a sharp-toothed mouth open in a terrifying grin.

One moment the second man was lying on the mosses, his upper body submerged. The next, he had been yanked into the pool with a mighty splash. He flailed in the silty spring water while something fey and sinuous wound about the man. A smack, a gulp, and the water stilled.

Brea had the sick knowledge that he would not rise again.

Carrig scrambled to his feet, looking into the spring with wide, fearful eyes. The leader's face grew pale, but neither of them made any move to go to their comrade's aid.

Not that they could have helped him. The power of mortal men was of little use when the spirits of a place took their revenge.

"I held him tight, I swear it," Carrig said. "Something pulled him under. You saw it."

"Aye," the black-haired man said. "Let's away from this foul place."

Brea gathered all her courage and briefly closed her eyes in a prayer of supplication. Her heart cried out to the spring and its guardians for succor, for mercy. This was her moment. Now, before the leader tightened his grip and they towed her away.

"Look!" she cried, pointing into the waters.

There was nothing to be seen—the drowned man had disappeared entirely, along with the water creature who had taken him. But it was distraction enough. The bandit holding her leaned forward, his grip slackening as he peered into the water.

Brea wrenched out of his grasp, took two steps, and leaped into the pool.

She let herself sink, expelling her precious air in a long stream of bubbles, a string of pearls reaching back toward the pale surface of the water. Dappled light sifted through the waters, though shadows gathered at the pool's edge. Her lungs went slack, then began to burn. She forced herself not to rise. Not to take a desperate, futile breath. The men waited up there for her, but she would never return.

Something cool brushed her fingers, and she turned herself about in the water, her long, dark hair swirling past her face.

It was the silver scale, coming as readily to her hand as it had eluded the brigand's. She smiled, tasting the clear, cool water against her teeth, and brought the scale to her heart.

Mother, I call upon your blood running salty in my veins. I call upon the ancient spirits of this watery haven. I call upon the hawthorn tree bound with wishes and the pale stars hidden behind the sunlit sky.

Take this human body and give it fins. Let me breathe water instead of air. Carry me away from the coarse hands of mortal men.

Her chest was full of coals, but she would not ascend back to the daylit world. Brea clenched her cold fingers, fighting to remain still. Submerged. Warm salt escaped her eyes and floated away, diluted to nothing. At last she could bear it no more, and drew in a great lungful of water.

As if waiting for that surrender, her body began to change. Her arms pulled in to her sides, her legs fused together. Her eyes shifted, her mouth pursed, the blood in her veins cooled even as her heartbeat surged. Liquid fire scalded every cell of her body as she transformed.

The surface of the spring shivered. A fey breeze stirred the wishing cloths tied to the hawthorn tree.

A heartbeat passed. A year, a day.

The girl-that-was flicked her tail and followed the shining current down and away. A thread of magic called her into the wild waters. Called her into the star-speckled, unchanging twilight far from any mortal shore. Called her home.

CHAPTER 2
PASSAGE

THE GIRL SAT UPON A STONE, dangling one leg into the water. Fish nibbled at her toes, heedless of the runes marking the rock. Her gossamer-spun dress reflected the sunset hues suspended between sky and wave.

The cool touch of the waves soothed her, though her mind was full of confusion. One moment her world had been full of splash and glimmer and then, mid-leap, something had changed. *She* had changed.

She'd had a name, once. It slipped, elusive as a minnow, into the shadowed corners of her mind, but she was determined to lure it out.

Tangled memory made her frown as she stared down into the waters. She was certain she had not always had legs. The lazy movements of the fish were as familiar to her—more familiar, in fact—than the sight of her own two hands. She held them up and stared at the long, unwebbed fingers. Who was she? *What* was she, and how had she come here?

A soft wind brushed strands of her dark hair across her face, and with the touch came remembrance.

Brea.

She was Brea Cairgead, fisherman's daughter. And daughter of a sea-wild woman who carried magic in her blood. Magic she'd given to her daughter, though it had come nearly too late.

Memory returned in a hot, painful rush, and Brea bent, arms wrapped across her stomach.

Her father was dead, her village had banished her, and she had barely managed to escape the brigands who had robbed her, and wished to do worse. The ache of remembrance washed over her in a heavy wave, but in its wake came gentler memories: the healing silver current, the sibilant songs of the sea, the cool touch of water cradling her.

Brea drew in a deep breath and straightened. Surely her life had held sorrow, but also peace. Now, though, what did the future hold? It was a very human thought, one that her finned self would never consider.

"Ah, she has awoken," a merry voice said. "Welcome to the Realm, sometime-girl."

Startled, Brea looked up to see a small fellow dressed in tatters and leaves sitting cross-legged upon the nearby bank. She opened her mouth, but the taste of words was foreign on her tongue, and the air rushed in, making her cough.

"Steady now," the figure said. "You're new enough into this form that you must go slowly. Allow me to introduce myself. I am the sprite called Puck."

He rose, then kept rising until he floated several hand spans above the grassy bank. Eyes twinkling, he bowed, turning the movement into a somersault in midair. Then he conjured a bright green hat with a jaunty plume. Jamming it over his tangled hair, he strode across the empty air between them until he was close enough to touch.

Brea shrank back on her rock and considered plunging

back below the surface. But this little fellow was, although a bit startling, not terribly frightening. Carefully, she rolled words out of her mouth.

"Where... am I?"

"As I said, you're in the Realm. The Realm of Faerie. Don't be afraid. You belong here, Mistress Brea Cairgead, silver fish girl, breather of both air and water."

She still wondered if she ought to slip off her rocky perch and into the cool, familiar safety of the water. It was home to her, more recently than the thatched cottage she'd once inhabited. She did not know how many turnings of the moon she'd spent in her other form, but she suspected the time could be measured in years. Perhaps decades. Yet something had prompted her transformation back to a human-seeming girl.

Magic, or fate, or even loneliness—she did not know which. Perhaps all three.

"Am I a faerie now?" she asked, afraid to hear the answer.

Puck tilted his head and regarded her a long moment, eyes bright. The wind riffled the surface of the water, and she smelled mint and thyme on the breeze.

"You are a curious creature," the sprite said. "You were never fully human, but you are human enough that you cannot entirely be one of the fey folk. As I said before, you are a girl of two parts—water and land, fey and mortal. As such, you have a part to play in things to come."

She did not like the sound of that. Brea hugged her knees close to her chest. "What if I do not want this fate?"

"What *do* you want?"

The answer was lodged in her heart, but she hesitated to speak it aloud. Still, Puck regarded her with kindness in his wild and merry eyes, and despite her wariness, she answered.

"To belong." It was what she'd always wanted, and what she'd never had.

Even as a village lass, she'd been too different. And now she realized there were none of her own kind. The selkies might tolerate her presence, but the merfolk would laugh at her ungainly human legs, and if she transformed she would not be able to speak with them.

"You have to make your own belonging," Puck said, a deep melancholy in his voice, as if he, too, were the only one of his kind.

Brea tasted salt in the back of her throat. She had no notion of how to fit herself into a world—whether human or faerie—that did not hold the shape of who she was.

"Do not despair." Puck shook himself, and she saw his sorrow fly off his shoulders and fade into the sunset sky. "If you are true of heart, you will find the way. Deep inside you, the path awaits."

"How will I know where to find it?"

"Follow the taste of the rowan berry," he said. "It will lead you to your fate. And now, Mistress Brea, I must bid you farewell."

"Don't go." She reached one pale hand toward him. Before he'd come, she had not known she was so lonely.

He did not reply—only spun himself about three times in a whirl of tatters and feathers and was gone.

Shore birds cried into the dusk, and the water lapped the bank. There was no one to talk to, except the school of silver fish swimming about the stone. And they did not speak in conversation, but in flashes of image and color.

Still, it was better than the silence of her own human thoughts. Letting out all her breath, Brea pushed herself off the rock and let the water surround her. Three heartbeats later there was no dark-haired girl pining upon a half-submerged stone, but only a new fish weaving through the current.

It was an unquiet current though, with an amber-gold thread of loam and smoke and shadows running through. It brushed along her sides, beckoning, and she found she could not resist its call.

Despite her efforts, she was not able to interest the other fish in following to see where it led. They desired only pale wave and lavender ripple, bright dart and flashing turn.

Alone, Brea-within-the-fish circled about her companions in farewell, and then left them to play in the light-filled shallows.

The taste of mystery pulled her on, past a rocky outcropping to a place where a stream poured into the larger water. Amber diluted with turquoise as the waters mixed and flowed, but it was that warmer taste within the rivulet that she must follow.

She dashed herself into the mouth of the stream and was pushed back. Once, twice, thrice—and then she discovered the trick of swimming against the current. First to one side and then the other she swam, stitching her way from bank to bank.

When she wearied she found a quiet eddy behind an algae-covered rock, and rested there until she regained her strength. The sky above the stream darkened as she followed the golden strand within the water, until at last she reached a small side-pool that tasted of contentment.

Flicking her tail, she dived in and out of the stream, but the golden thread had curled in on itself and gone to rest in the silty bottom. The undercut bank held peaceful shadows, and the tangled roots of trees wove a screen she might shelter behind. It was as good enough a place as any to bide.

Overhead, the evergreens nodded, their branches waving

softly like a mother hushing her child. Above their dark heads the first sprinkling of stars shone, flecks of light springing up before the sickle moon could scythe them down.

There was no passage of days in the waters where Brea now dwelt. The sky dimmed and brightened from dusk to night and back again, skipping sunlight altogether. She discovered the rocks upstream where the current frothed and raced, and the quiet eddies where tadpoles fluttered. When the moon shone full, dew-winged sprites danced above the silver-lit stream, their footsteps light as rain over the water.

Brea felt no urge to move on. The golden strand that had brought her here did not reappear to beckon her forth to new rivers and depths. She splashed and darted, waiting without urgency for whatever might come. Some deep sense of knowing told her she was where she ought to be.

That peaceful contentment changed one dusky evening. The evergreens shivered, and she felt their roots stirring in the water.

Something was coming.

She darted beneath the bank and held herself there, suspended. Watching.

Brightness approached—a ball of flame hovering and bobbing through the forest. It halted on the opposite side of the stream, licking the surface with streaks of red and gold. She was too afraid to rise and see if it were a wisp, or a fallen star, or a light held aloft by some strange creature.

Sound filtered through the water, syllables with edges, full of question and danger. Brea back-finned into the shadows.

She would hide until the forest became quiet and safe once more.

As if sensing her movement, the ball of flame floated out to the middle of the stream. Brea whirled and darted deeper beneath the bank, though she feared it was already too late.

After a dozen of her frightened heartbeats, the fiery sphere withdrew. It moved along the bank a short distance, but she knew the danger was not over. Indeed, the light returned soon enough, and the soil vibrated with the sound of footsteps. More than one creature roamed there beside the stream. They seemed to be seeking something.

A berry floated past, carried gently on top of the water. Brea ignored it and practiced blending with the roots she sheltered behind.

Another came past, and another, each one leaving a trace of flavor behind—something wild and tangy. *Freedom. Adventure. Come, bite.* The berries bobbed on the surface, red and full of magic.

She must not taste of them. Brea forced herself to stay in the deeps, her body quivering with effort.

A dozen floated slowly by, one by one. At the thirteenth, she could remain still no longer. Despairing, she flipped her body upward, capturing the berry in her mouth.

The taste trembled through her, urgent and immediate. Without letting it go, she fled downstream. Something pulled taut, then let her run, then wound up again. The far bank drew nearer, but she could not release the fruit. It was stuck fast in her mouth, and so she darted and ran, seeking vainly to escape.

The flame bobbed directly overhead, a tiny sun. She broke the surface in a panic of air and silver, twisting desperately. The light suffocated her and she thrashed, trying to break free.

Then darkness closed about her, but it was not the comforting liquid of the shadows. This was rough and dry, scraping her skin, smelling of something horrible. Harsh air surrounded her, and Brea gasped, drowning in the dryness...

Change. She must shift her form, or die.

Summoning all her strength, she bid her body to transform. Hard earth beneath her. Not water. *No longer fish, but girl*. She clung to the thought, and at last her scales fell away. Pain rippled through her as she became heavy and slow, trapped by air and gravity, now elongated into her human form.

It was done—but she was still in darkness. Drawing in shallow, rapid breaths, she realized she was caught in folds of cloth. She clawed at the fabric until she was free.

Trees above her, and the orb of the moon. Beyond lay the safety of the stream—but two creatures stood between her and the water. Not monsters. Humans, but so strangely garbed.

One of them stepped forward, hair an odd, bright color, and said something that might have been a greeting.

Or a threat.

The other set one hand to his belt, where a knife hung.

Brea glanced down at her own form. She was naked, her long dark hair woven with white blossoms. *Run!*

A heartbeat later she was on her feet, leaping surefooted through the forest. If she could loop back around to the stream, or even find a pond, she could dive for safety.

Behind her the humans crashed and called.

Brea lifted her face, scenting the wind for water. Something golden and sweet tugged at her senses and she veered, leaping lightly over bracken fern. Despite her nakedness, the forest was kind. The moss cushioned her steps, and no sharp twigs scraped her pale unprotected skin.

The forest thinned, the scent drawing her on. A half-remembered taste, tart and lovely. Apples.

She broke out of the trees into silvery grasses dancing in the starlight. Before her rose a long hill, and at the top a tree grew, branches heavy with both blossom and fruit. She cast a glance behind her, to see her pursuers closer than she had guessed.

With a last burst of speed, Brea raced up the hill. The apple tree bowed and bent, a golden fruit caught high in its branches, but she dared not pause.

Onward, past the tree, past a faerie ring studded with mushrooms, past a low stone wall. At last, breath scraping in her lungs, limbs burning with effort, she could run no more.

There was no lake, no stream, no rivulet nearby to offer her shelter. Wearily, Brea dropped to the ground, the grasses rising around her. At least the human creatures no longer chased her. The silence of the night was broken only by the chirp of an insect, the rustle of the wind through the grass.

And then came a sound to freeze her newly-warmed blood: the wail of a hunting horn echoing across the sky.

The Wild Hunt was riding.

Even safe in her waterborne form, she knew to dive deep when the unearthly riders and spectral hounds galloped through the night. Once, she had seen the wavering shadow of the Huntsman silhouetted against the moon, his fearsome shape crowned with mighty antlers.

Shivering, Brea stood and scanned the silvery meadows surrounding her. Far ahead a dark smudge rose on the horizon; perhaps a sheltering forest, perhaps a low rise of hills. She lifted her face and scented deeply of the air, but there was no smell of water nearby. No safety she could plunge into and disappear.

She prayed there was still some cover she might find, a hazel copse or small tarn. Turning her steps toward the horizon, she began to run once more.

The horn did not sound again, but far too soon she heard the shrill yipping of hounds and the thunder of hooves. Brea glanced over her shoulder and gasped at the sight of the Wild Hunt galloping across the sky, bearing down on her in all their glory.

Glowing, gossamer-maned horses with fiery eyes bore stern and beautiful elfin knights, their hair whipping in the wind. Hounds raced before them, sinuous as smoke, red eyes burning like coals. And in the midst, the horned figure of the Huntsman, a midnight cloak billowing behind him.

Heart beating fast as a bird's, Brea raced over the meadows. Above the sharpness of her breaths and the drumming hooves, she heard the high keening of bagpipes.

There was no escape. She was too slow, and the hunt surrounded her.

The riders landed, hemming her in a circle, and Brea halted. Chin high, she faced the Huntsman, though her legs felt weak as water.

"What do you want of me?" she asked.

"The Dark Queen demands your presence," the Huntsman said, his voice deep and low. "You have aided the enemy."

"What enemy?" She cast her mind back, trying to understand, but his words had no meaning. Did this concern the humans who had chased her? "I have done nothing."

"That is for the queen to decide."

The horned figure gestured to one of his riders. Before Brea could utter a protest she was scooped up and set in front of a black-haired rider with cold green eyes. His arm was a vise about her waist, and she did not bother to struggle. She would conserve her strength for a fight that she might win.

Although how she could possibly win anything from the Dark Queen of the Realm, Brea had no notion. She knew very little about the queen, having never strayed far into the midnight side of the Realm. Neither had she forayed into the sunlit reaches ruled by the Bright King. The dusk-lit sky had been enough for her, the sunset-tipped waves and still pools lit silver by the rising moon.

All she knew was that the queen ruled the Dark Realm, and that even in the gloaming far from the midnight heart of her court, creatures spoke of her with fear and awe.

The eldritch horn sounded, and the Wild Hunt leaped into the sky. The air cooled and the wind of their passing blew Brea's dark hair back from her face. Around them, the stars hovered close as the fiery-footed steeds climbed into the sky. She felt as though she might lift her hand and cut her fingers against the sickle blade of the moon.

Night wove thickly about the hunt as they rode into the heart of the Dark Realm, until at last they reached the stillness of midnight. Gnarled oaks grew in the shadowed forest below, and she glimpsed a clearing lit with dozens of faerie-fire candles and a bonfire flickering with purple light.

Fey folk thronged there, some dancing wildly about the violet flames, others gathered at the long feasting tables set at one side of the clearing. She blinked to see so many creatures: dream-winged faerie maids and sharp-toothed nixies, a bone-white shadow inside a dark cloak, the wide-eyed stare of the banshee.

Music drifted above the tangled treetops—harp and drum and guitar twining together, sorrowful and joyous in equal measure. The Wild Hunt followed the melody down and landed in the center of the clearing.

At the far end stood a throne of vines and thorns, and upon it sat the Dark Queen. Her hair was smoke and obsidian, her gown starlight and cobwebs, and her eyes held the memory of countless centuries.

Brea swallowed, her throat dry with fear as the elfin knight set her on the mossy ground. Her legs trembled, and she looked down to see she was clad once more in a shimmer of a gown that clung to her like mist.

"Huntsman," the queen said. "Have you brought me the betrayer?"

"I have, your majesty." He made her a sweeping bow. "This maid is the one we scented, who led the humans directly to the tree of the golden apple."

Brea's skin prickled with fear, and she sucked in a painful breath. "I did not—"

"You." The queen's voice cut like frost. She leaned forward and pointed at Brea with one long, pale finger. "I should strike you down where you stand for aiding my enemies."

Brea had never meant to lead the humans anywhere, but only to escape. Had she done something terrible, all unwitting?

"Forgive me, your majesty," she whispered.

A bright-eyed, tangle-haired sprite tumbled into the clearing before the Dark Queen's throne. Brea recognized him —Puck, who spoke in riddles and runes. Standing before the queen, he made his ruler a flourishing bow, one foot pointed on the velvet green mosses.

"Your majesty," he said. "Might I speak?"

The queen let out a sigh, the sound like a wind stirring the empty branches of winter oaks.

"Puck," she said. "You have the freedom of the courts, much as it may displease my mood. Say your piece."

"Yon maid, all unwitting, played but a part in a quest. She does not deserve death—and there are few enough fey folk that her loss, though a small thing, would be felt within the realm."

Brea sent him a grateful glance. She did not know why Puck was defending her. Perhaps it had to do with their prior meeting and his cryptic words of fate and future.

"Banishment, then, shall be her punishment," the queen declared. "To the Shadowlands."

The denizens of the court shivered, and Brea felt her heart catch. Even hiding within her watery dwelling, she'd heard of that dire place where souls wandered, lost and alone, into eternity.

Though the words might stumble on her tongue, she must plead her case.

"My queen." She bowed as best she could on her unsteady legs. "I beg you, do not banish me. Surely there is some way to mend the harm I might have done?"

The gathered fey folk whispered, and Brea was glad she could not hear what they said. No doubt they suggested dire and dreadful remedies.

"Perchance there might be." The queen narrowed her eyes and gestured. "Bard Thomas, attend."

A man stepped from the shadows and Brea stared at him in surprise. Another half-magical human like herself, perhaps? But no—there was something ghostly about him. If he'd been human once, he was no longer. Silver strands ran through his brown hair, and his eyes were wise and weary beyond measure.

"Yes, my queen?"

"How best might I use this youngling in service to the court?"

The man turned, his gaze brushing past Puck and then resting upon Brea for a long moment. Sparks and promises flashed in his eyes, and she did not know whether to be hopeful or afraid.

"Send her into the human world," he said at last. "There, she might sway mortals to stray into the Realm. She can repay her debt by helping ensure that humans will cross over to the Dark Court when they enter the game of Feyland."

The queen gave a single shake of her head. "I mislike having to sacrifice yet another of my handmaidens simply to send a near-useless creature into the mortal realm. Your counsel pleases me not, bard."

"Milady." Puck sprang into the air and hovered there. "Though centuries have passed, the girl *is* part human, and still connected with the mortal world. I may be able to slip her through the gateway without further bloodshed. And if not"—he gave an elaborate shrug—"then do with her as you please."

"Your magic is fickle," the queen said.

"Yet you know it cannot be forced to do your bidding." Puck laughed and flipped in the air, landing once again on the soft ground. "I will attempt to send the maid through."

The queen leaned back, the pale moonlight illuminating her beauty. Overhead, stars sprinkled the edges of the sky, and a night wind stirred the oak leaves into whispering. Brea's nerves hummed as she awaited her fate. Her heartbeat pounded within her chest until she was nearly dizzy from the rhythm, yet she remained quiet and still, as she had learned to do in her watery form. Speaking on her own behalf would do little good, and she did not want to tip the balance of the queen's decision unfavorably.

At length the queen beckoned to Brea, who found she could not ignore the summons. She came forward, then sank to her knees on the velvety mosses before the throne.

"I lay a *geas* upon you, youngling," the Dark Queen said. "From now until the summer wanes, you are charged with marking and leading as many humans as you might toward the magic of the Dark Court so that the Realm may be replenished. Should you return without success, the Shadowlands will be your new home."

Brea bowed her head. There was no arguing, and no agreement. When the queen spoke, her word was law. Still, this sentence was a reprieve. If she carried out the queen's bidding well enough, she might escape dire banishment to the Shadowlands.

Behind the tangled throne, gossamer-winged faerie maidens cast Brea pitying glances. A nearby band of goblins cackled, clearly pleased by her plight. The queen held up one hand and called forth her magic. In a burst of violet light, a silver medallion appeared. It swung, dangling on a bright chain from the queen's fingers.

"Take this," she said, thrusting the medallion at Brea. "It is your passage back to the realm—but do not call upon it until Lughnasa is nigh."

Brea took the medallion. It was cool against her fingers, the silver disc inset with a pale moonstone, the edges inscribed with runes. She folded it into her palm, proof of the journey she must now undertake.

"Away with her," the queen said to Puck.

Without a further glance at Brea, she signaled for elderberry wine and music. The creatures of her court bestirred themselves, returning to their dancing and feasting.

"Come, maid," Puck said.

Brea rose and followed him. She did not look behind her as they left the clearing of the Dark Court, though the strains of a plaintive jig followed her into the shimmering darkness beneath the trees.

"I am afraid," she said, once the sounds of the court had faded.

"You are wise to be so," Puck said. "Yet who knows what doors will open to you in the human world, or what fate might hold in store?"

She did not want fate or a queen's commands to rule her—but she had no choice.

Puck led her along mossy paths faintly illuminated with starshine. Overhead, the dark oaks wove their tangled branches across the star-dappled sky.

"Quickly," the sprite urged. "We must slip you through before the battle commences. I have folded time, but we must make haste."

Brea gulped back her questions. She doubted she wanted to know the answers. Battle? Folded time? Instead she quickened her pace, until she and Puck were nearly flying through the forest. Or perhaps they truly were airborne. Her feet did not seem to touch the ground, and she would not be surprised if the sprite's magic propelled them forward. Overhead, the sky lightened to a pearly grey.

"Here." Puck halted before a strange clearing, still floating in the air. "We are in time."

Brea's feet landed on the cool moss, and she blinked at the clearing. It was not a single glade, but three, lined up like a triple reflection. The one nearest them held a faerie ring of moon-pale mushrooms, the far one was lit by morning sun and its circle made of white-speckled red mushrooms, and the one in the middle was a mixture of both—sun and shadow, pale mushrooms and red growing together to make the faerie ring.

Puck strode to the middle clearing and flourished his fingers in a strange gesture. Colored mist began forming in the center of the faerie ring—golden and violet and emerald swirling together.

"Keep the medallion safe," the sprite said, nodding to the silver pendant still clutched in her hand. "And remember your name, for moving between the worlds, much as shifting your shape, can cause a clouding of the spirit. Step into the mist, and be brave."

She was not brave, nor had she ever been. She'd merely done what had to be done—which seemed to take her only from one trouble to the next.

"What must I do, once I reach the human world?" she asked, slowly walking toward the bright eddies of mist.

"Mark humans with a touch of faerie magic, so that they are called into the Realm," Puck said. "But most of all, trust your heart."

The sprite ever spoke in riddles, with few answers. She let out a low sigh.

Beside them, the clearing holding the moon-pale ring began to glow. Puck gave it a wary glance, then gestured at her to hurry.

"Farewell, Maid Brea," he said. "Luck be upon you."

She hoped the fates heard his words.

"Farewell, Puck."

Gathering the shreds of her courage, she stepped into the swirling mist of the center clearing. The world tipped, dizziness pouring over her until she fell to her knees. She could feel the sweet magic of the Realm of Faerie ripping away, and she cried out from the pain of it.

It was not the first time she'd been pulled from one world to another, though, and she vowed that whatever happened, she would survive this transformation.

Human or faerie, she would stay true to her word. And perhaps, one day, she would find her way home. Wherever that might be.

CHAPTER 3
ARRIVAL

THE FAERIE MAID ARRIVED in a bubble of cold blue light, a barrier between herself and the dangers of the mortal world. Before she could take a breath the magic dissipated, revealing crumbling structures and pitted pavement beneath a dimly-lit sky. She shivered as the clammy air pressed against her skin. It seemed to be night, though there was no moon to guide her, no pinpricks of stars shining steady overhead.

The air smelled wrong, tainted with rot and strange metallic fumes. The light was peculiar too, an orange wash smeared across the clouds. But the sounds were the most foreign things: monstrous growls approaching and receding, mortal voices raised in shouts of fear or anger, the rushing pulse of something too mechanical to be waves pushing against the shore.

In one hand she clutched a silver medallion inset with a moonstone, the chain trickling through her fingers. More than a talisman, it was a means to return back to the enchanted world from which she had come. Precious beyond words.

She had arrived with a reason, a *geas* set upon her. And she must remember...

Remember her name.

Blinking, she tried to recall it. Her human name, which once she had worn as easily as a woolen shawl wrapped about her shoulders. Once—before she had plunged into the Realm of Faerie and lost all need for human things.

The sound of her name slipped through the shadows of her memory, an elusive silver fish, darting away. She pressed her lips together, trying to recall the shape of it.

Brea. That had been her name.

Brea Cairgead.

She whispered it softly, reclaiming the taste of it in her mouth. She was Brea, now, no longer a moonbeam swimming beneath the waters. And along with the awkward syllables, she now wore an equally clumsy form.

She stood unsteadily on her two human legs and tried to quell the nervousness prickling through her. The wrongness of this world made her heart beat fast, her gossamer garment no protection from the night. Every instinct shouted at her to flee, to flick her tail and dart to the concealing coolness of the deep shadows.

Yet even if there had been a sheltering pool nearby, she was trapped in this mortal shape. There would be no tail, no fins, no undulating through the bright waters. Not until she completed her quest and was allowed to return home to the Realm of Faerie.

Ah, but she was so weak compared to most members of the Dark Court. Their mocking words still echoed in her thoughts.

"That one?" The black-mouthed banshee had shrieked with glee. "She'll not last a day in the human world!"

"Aye, she'll be eaten in a trice." One of the redcap goblins licked his lips, then bared his needle-sharp teeth. "Maybe I'll follow her in and do the job."

"No need," a fungal-covered hooligan sneered. "She'll return defeated by the next moon, mark my words. Then the queen might give her to you as a plaything."

The Dark Queen's cold voice had cut through the babble. "This maid betrayed the Realm, and must pay the price. Whether she succeeds or not, I lay this geas upon her. Should she fail, she shall be banished to walk the Shadowlands forever."

The court had tittered at the queen's words. Their bright, avid gazes had fixed on Brea, anticipating her disgraceful return, ready to revel in the crushing bitterness of her failure.

She must not fail.

Though she might have been fully mortal once, was she not now a creature of the Realm? She had a few small magics to call upon, paltry though they might be. Lifting her face to the absent moon, she prayed they would be enough.

She was alone and afraid, but she would not let this strange new place defeat her. Brea pulled in a breath of tainted air, trying not to cough at the sour taste. First, she must find a safe haven. Once hidden, she could begin to explore this city of the humans, fortify herself, and discover a way to fulfill the queen's commands.

Something moved in the shadowed mouth of a nearby alleyway.

"Well, well. What's a pretty thing like you doing out here in the Exe?" The voice was smooth and full of menace.

Brea whirled, breath clogging in her throat, to see a pock-faced man leaning against the crumbling wall. His smile and the blade of his knife glinted in the dim light. From down the alley came the clack of rubble dislodged and soft footsteps. Two more men emerged, young and feral-looking.

Any brief notion that she might be able to use these humans fled. She was prey here, not predator.

"Only wearing a nightie, too." The first man's smile widened. "Sleepwalking, love? We can show you back to bed."

The others laughed, something brutish in the sound.

"What's in her hand?" one of them asked.

The first man straightened and began to approach. "Are you a runaway, been stealing jewelry? Let's have a look."

No. She could not lose the medallion.

Brea gulped air, then turned and ran. Blindly, stupidly, stumbling over discarded metal pipes that burned her bare feet. Behind her came the sounds of pursuit, the men tossing banter back and forth. There was no doubt they would catch her.

Moon and stars, please let her find a safe place!

A noisesome puddle slicked her feet with oil, and she scraped her arm upon a coil of sharp wire. Tears leaked from the corners of her eyes.

Heart hammering, she veered around a corner, then let out a cry of relief. A tree stood in an abandoned square ahead, branches reaching into the eerie orange sky. She forced herself to run faster, and heard her pursuers accelerate in response. Closer, closer...

Gasping, she fetched up at the tree, her hands going to the rough bark for reassurance. For power.

She cried out again, but not in relief. The tree was dead, a husk with withered roots reaching into the poisoned soil. There was no living energy she could pull forth to help her defeat her enemies. Only soot and dust.

The men rushed up and surrounded her, the leader coming to stand before her.

"Enough," he said. His breath came easy in his chest, and Brea bitterly rued her new human form, that could scarcely run a handful of minutes without tiring.

He caught her wrist, and she yelped at the touch of metal against her skin. Bright spots of pain drilled into her body from where his iron-ringed hand clasped her arm, and she yanked herself free, medallion still gripped tightly in her closed fist.

Brea closed her eyes briefly, old fear washing through her. She had been chased by brigands one fateful day, long ago. Caught then, too. But this time there was no silent, sacred water waiting to welcome her in. No liquid transformation that could be wrought.

"Take her back to the rest of the pack?" one of the younger men asked.

"Head Jackal will want to see what we caught," the first man said. "Too bad she don't have a wrist chip. Looks more valuable than she is. Though whatever she's got..."

He grabbed her again, and pried her fingers open. The silver medallion was revealed upon her palm, gleaming in the faint light. The runes inscribed on the surface were barely visible, but the moonstone shone as if lit from within.

Despair washed through her, but she pushed it away. She *must* escape. She had no choice.

And, despite what she appeared, she was not simply a frightened mortal girl, unaware of her own magic. She was a creature of Faerie, one of the fey folk.

Unfortunately, the medallion she held was no use, despite the powerful spell it contained. The talisman's magic could not be turned to any purpose but the one it was made for—to send her back to the Dark Court. Should she return now, her fate would be sealed. A goblin's plaything, then eternal banishment to a land of dust and shadows.

"Pretty." The man reached to pluck it from her hand.

Heart pounding in her chest, Brea closed her fingers around the medallion. Fiercely, she summoned the power of the invisible stars, the small, rugged weeds pushing up through cracks in the paving, the salty rush of blood under the men's skin.

Glimmer and fade, come to my aid. Mortal flesh turn to air, bear me safe away from here.

She half closed her eyes and willed herself to become a wisp of shadow, a tatter of moonlight. The dead tree pulsed and shivered, the weeds on the sidewalk wilted over, spent. A violent shiver wracked her body, and then she disappeared, her form now invisible, yet still present.

A breath of wind curled around the dead tree, and she caught the tail of it and let it pull her out of reach.

"Where'd she go?" the first man yelled.

"You were supposed to be holding her," one of the youths said.

"She was right here, dammit. Don't just stand there, find her."

They split up, searching the shadows, their footsteps angry over the ground. They would not catch her. Already she was slipping beyond their reach, carried away on the breeze.

"Take me to a safe haven," she whispered, fighting her body's urge to become solid once more.

Not yet. She must find a hiding place.

The wind eddied and turned, bearing her first high, then low. Lights of human habitation spread like a blanket, but the place she was traveling over was dark. That would serve well enough—for was she not a creature who dwelt on the edge of the Dark Realm? Here in the mortal world, darkness would be her ally.

At last the breeze slid through the broken-out window of an abandoned building. Thrice around it went, like an animal making its den, then whispered away to nothing.

Unable to maintain her ethereal state, Brea tumbled to the cold cement floor and landed painfully on her hands and knees. She shuddered, breathing fast to combat the sudden sickness in her belly. Curses upon this ungainly human body she now wore, bound by gravity and bone.

Finally, the feeling passed and she sat up, alert for any sign of danger.

The growls and rumbles of mortal machines were distant here, muted to a dull ache. She sensed no trace of the men who'd tried to ensnare her. Other humans dwelt near to her hiding place—she could feel the sickly yellow pulse of their presence—but they were wounded and worn, presenting no immediate threat.

Exhaustion crashed down on her like the flume of a waterfall. The medallion slipped gently from her hand and clinked upon the cement.

She was safe—for now.

Thirst burned through her, waking her from confused dreams of the Dark Queen's midnight gaze, Puck's impish smile.

But she was no longer in the Realm, as her aching mortal body proved.

Water.

The need pushed her to her feet, and she stood a moment,

surveying her hiding place. The silver medallion lay gleaming against the cracked, stained floor. She picked it up, magicked a pocket into her gossamer garment, and tucked the talisman away.

Wan yellow light crept in through the broken doorway, spilled over the jutting overhang of the ruined roof. The sky overhead was blue, and she caught her breath. For so long she had lived in the sweet dimness of the Dusk Vale, she'd nearly forgotten the color of the daytime sky.

The sight gave her the strength to step over the rubbled threshold. Outside, another dead tree rose beside the wall of her shelter, its dry, dead leaves whispering together in the faint breeze. The air smelled of decay and things long abandoned.

She turned in a slow circle, examining the half-ruined building, the withered tree, the broken walkway where thin grasses struggled up between the cracks.

Yes. This place would serve as her temporary home.

There was much to do in order to make it a place of some comfort, but first she must find water.

The oil-slimed puddles she sensed in a nearby alleyway made her wrinkle her nose in disgust. No, she could not stomach such tainted liquid. She closed her eyes and hummed softly. *Cool water, pure water, whither might you be?*

The shimmer of an answer came from deeper inside her shelter, though it was masked with the forbidding hum of iron. Brea followed the song into a small room where tiny insects scuttled. A white trough lay within, and a smaller basin. The scent of water rose strongly from the walls.

How to reach it?

She folded her arms and studied the basin, reluctantly coming to the conclusion that the metal handles protruding from the wall would release the water. Yet she could not touch them without burning herself.

"Think, girl," she said, the sound of her own voice soft in the dimness.

Back in the main room, she cast about for an answer. The tiny red heartbeats of small rodents pulled her to the far corner, where mice nested in a pile of torn rags.

"I am sorry," she said to them, "but I'm in need of your bedding. Perhaps you ought to find another dwelling place."

She did not particularly relish the thought of sharing her new quarters with the mice, anyway. Using a bit of magic, she nudged them forth, a half-dozen furry, squeaking bodies that made for the door without much protest.

Gingerly picking up the rags, Brea carried them to the doorway and shook them vigorously. Despite her weakness, she laid a quick cleansing enchantment upon the dingy bits of cloth. The effort left her shaking, and she leaned against the doorjamb for a long moment, letting the pale sun warm her skin.

Water.

Yes, yes. Somewhat unsteadily she went back into the small room. Gritting her teeth at the painful proximity of cold iron, she wrapped the rags about one handle, and turned. It squeaked with disuse, and a coughing rattle came from within the walls.

A trickle emerged, stained with minerals, and Brea turned the handle harder. *Please.*

Glorious fresh water spilled forth into the basin.

She turned her face to the sky, to the invisible stars, and breathed a prayer of thanks. Then, careful to avoid the spigot, she stuck her hands into that life-giving stream and gulped greedily from her cupped palms. Peace and strength flowed into her. Smiling, she leaned forward and let the water run over her head, down into her eyes and grateful mouth.

At last, replete, she shut the water off and shook her wet hair away from her face. Now she could start exploring her surroundings and make a plan of action. For the first time, a flutter of excitement went through her.

It had been a long, long time since she'd inhabited the human world. And although she was a fey creature now, there was, perhaps, a kernel of loneliness in her heart. An ache belonging to the mortal part of herself, whether she wanted it or not.

But yearnings aside, she needed to ward her shelter for safety and protection. With renewed magic coursing through her, she hummed and wove her spells. First, a layer of aversions strung like spider silk around the perimeter, so that any human wandering by would have no interest in exploring further, and would turn away.

Then more protections about the threshold and broken windows, and where the roof gaped open, keeping away anything that would mean her harm.

It was not the kind of magic that would leap and attack, like a guard dog, but a deflection—a pebble placed in the current, that the water might run around without causing any harm.

Once her wards were complete she could no longer ignore the fact that she must now venture into the human world. She would need a disguise, of course, a glamour to pull across her features. Judging by the events of last night, it would need to be something fierce and forbidding.

After a moment's pondering, she combined the worst features of her three pursuers into one hulking, ugly human male, and let the guise settled over her shoulders.

Then, ignoring the tremor in her belly, she stepped out into the light.

As she had thought, the area around her shelter was mostly deserted. She turned toward the hum, the heartbeat of the city, and began to walk.

Two blocks down the empty street she passed a building filled with the sluggish dreams of yellow-eyed men. Their thoughts put her in mind of a nest of chilled wasps; slow to rouse, but once angered, difficult to escape. She resolved to give them a wide berth.

Further on, a hollow-cheeked woman rummaged through a pile of trash on the street. She shrank back as Brea strode past, fear rising off her in sour waves.

The sounds of human machines grew louder. Brea hesitated at the edge of an area pulsing with angry red light, invisible to the mortal gaze. This was the province of the men who had wanted to capture her, their territory marked by sigils painted on the nearby buildings—angular and bright, and full of warning.

She stood a moment, then turned aside. Even in her forbidding human guise, she would not be able to pass safely through.

Sooner than she was ready for, she went from the crumbling neighborhood into more normal human habitation. First, a few scrawny children who darted into sagging houses at her approach, then men gathered about hulks of painful iron in the street, then women moving hurriedly, bags of provisions beneath their arms.

Ahead the rush and roar grew louder, as did the vibrations of cold iron grating against her bones. When she came to the source, she stopped dead in surprise.

Horseless wagons made of metal charged up and down the

streets, growling and emitting noxious fumes. Humans rode inside, hurtling at abnormal speeds. Brea's belly clenched at the thought of being enclosed in so much iron.

The tang of it in the air smote her, and she swayed, dizziness shading her vision. Her mind darted this way and that, a minnow trapped in a puddle. She was defenseless, prey for any passing hunger.

Breathing shallowly through her mouth, she whirled and ran back the way she had come. Past the women and men, past the startled children, until enough crumbling brick and concrete was between her and the inimical hum of the metal.

Panting, she stopped beside a brightly painted wall and bent, hands on her knees. This would never do. How could she perform her task and obey the queen's bidding when she was overcome the moment she stepped into the heart of the human city? Already she could hear the mocking titters of the Dark Court denizens.

Think, girl, she told herself. Despite the general disbelief in her abilities, surely the Dark Queen would not have sent her on an entirely fruitless endeavor.

Which meant that, somehow, she had the strength to succeed.

Mortals did not feel the effect of cold iron. Once, she'd been one of them. She did not think she could ever be completely human, not after she had discovered her own magic and dwelt so long in the Realm; centuries, judging by the world she now found herself in.

But perhaps she might be able to become *more* human.

Not here, though, in an alleyway where she could still hear the roar of the metal contraptions. Shoulders slumped, she picked her way back into the Exe and the bare welcome of the shelter she had claimed as her own.

It took three days and three nights for her to find the balance.

The first day, she opened the hole in her heart, the one filled with human sorrow and loss, and dived in.

Her skin tightened and burned, her vision narrowed, the colors fading, and she could no longer feel the slow, steady pulse of the earth and stars. She stared at her blunt, human hands, smelled the stink of mortal fear, and panicked revulsion rose in her throat, nearly choking her.

No. Too much of herself was imbued with magic. Without it, she became nothing but a feeble human girl. As such, it would be impossible to carry out the queen's bidding. With great relief, she backed away from the edge of mortality. Cool silver closed over her, like the waters of a still pool, and she collapsed, exhausted, upon the hard floor.

She woke, aching, with the light of a new dawn. The concrete was cold beneath her, and the need for water burned her throat. Wincing, she rose and went to the bathing room. Clearly she'd gone too far into her own humanity the day before.

The water ran clear, and she caught some in a broken cup she had found the previous day on her way home. As she drank, careful of the jagged porcelain edge, she pondered.

What if she embraced her heritage, the shapechanging magic borne in her blood?

If this attempt went awry as the last one had, she should ensure there was sufficient water at hand. It would be the utmost stupidity to die flopping about the floor, suffocating from the harsh air.

She cobbled together a rough plug for the bathing trough, then filled it halfway with water. Perched on the side, she began to hum a liquid lullaby. Although she'd never met her mother, the woman had gifted her with the power to transform. Her mother's heritage was tied to the sea, but Brea had been unable to activate her own ability within the salty brine.

Instead, the pure water of the sacred spring had seen her first transformation. That location, and her half-human blood, might explain why she was not a mer-creature—nor a nixie, a water hag, or a nymph. Instead she was a girl who might become a flashing silver fish from one heartbeat to the next.

With that thought, she changed, slipping down into the water. There were no sheltering shadows, no waving tendrils of plants, no swirling currents to soothe her scales. Only plain water, carrying an unpleasant tang to her piscean senses, though it was safe enough for her to drink.

A sigh became bubbles, and then she sat in the water, human once more. Her gossamer dress clung wetly to her legs, and her hair dripped down her back.

Transforming to her fish form was no answer, either, though she felt much refreshed. Still, a silver trout could not do as the queen commanded.

Neither could an aching and non-magical human body.

Frowning, Brea rose from the tub. Despite her makeshift stopper, the water was slowly slipping down the drain. She tugged the plug out, then went to the main room of her shelter, leaving a trail of droplets in her wake.

If she were to embrace a greater degree of mortality, she would need more than a hard floor in an empty room. Such austerity was all very well for creatures of shadow and starlight, or fish who could swim away and find a home in any watery embrace. But for the magical mortal she must become, some comfort was in order.

She settled cross-legged on the stained cement, calling up memories of when she was human.

A bed was a necessity, and not just a thin straw mattress covered with a scratchy woolen blanket that still smelled of sheep. She would need clothing, and something to store it in. Someplace safe to keep the medallion—a small chest, perhaps—that she might bespell with protections. A drinking vessel that did not threaten to cut her mouth with each sip. Those would make a fine start.

And how will you insinuate yourself into the human world and begin the queen's quest? She banished the voice, though it caused a flutter of fear in her chest. First things first.

Now, while the strength of her magic flowed through her, she should attempt going among mortals again. But not on foot, and not into the area she had tried before.

She hummed again, and let herself become light as a wisp, a glimmer. *Breeze, bear me forth, high and safe overhead, to find what I seek, garments bright—and a bed.*

Clumsy, perhaps, but adequate. No one at the Dark Court had accused her of elegance in her spellcasting.

The obliging wind floated her up and out of the gap in her crumbling roof. From a height, the blight spreading over the Exe was plain. Decay, neglect, and loneliness—the ideal place to hide. She floated south, then east, trusting the air to carry her. Indeed, it was a much better solution than donning a glamour and trying to navigate the human world on foot. A pity she could not set her magical mark upon the mortals as she drifted past, but this form had its limitations.

She realized her mistake as she hovered before a window made of glass so smooth it was nearly invisible. Displayed inside were various items of clothing, some of them so garishly colored they assaulted her senses.

As a wisp of wind, she could not touch anything. Which meant she could not carry away garments, or bedding, or any of her purchases whatsoever.

But at least she could find the location of the vendors of such things. Perhaps even more importantly, she might observe the humans going about their business. The metal vehicles did not weaken her as much as they had the day before. She was growing stronger, and her ephemeral form seemed to buffer her from the worst effects.

A woman wearing a green coat passed beneath her. Brea caught the fragrance of lemon and spices in her hair, and decided to follow.

As luck would have it, the woman entered one of the shops lining the street. Brea managed to drift inside before the strange glass doors whooshed shut. Then she paused, glad she had no lungs, for she would have gasped aloud.

Row upon row of skirts and trousers, dresses and scarves; more than a hundred people could wear in a lifetime. Beyond the ranks of clothing stood cases overflowing with jewelry, colorful gems glinting amid the sheen of precious metals. And beyond even that, like some palace filled with wonders, dozens of beds, each one made up more opulently than the last.

The sheer abundance was dizzying. Chieftains of old would have fallen weeping to their knees, or gone to war a thousand times over for a fraction of the wealth on display.

"Look, mama." A young child holding her mother's hand, pointed to where Brea hovered near bank of lights. "Sparkly!"

"Yes, dear." The distracted parent didn't bother glancing up.

Even if she had, would she have seen Brea's shimmer? Unwilling to risk the chance, she wafted away toward the beds. She passed a corner filled with goblets and ornate plates, and an area where intricately patterned rugs spilled carelessly across the floor.

A constant ringing noise pulled her to an intersection in the center of the vast store. From her vantage point overhead, she watched as busy shop girls imprisoned behind a counter placed the various customers' goods into bags.

She drifted closer, trying to determine the system of payment. Certainly there was no barter here, no exchanging a bag of onions for a length of woven cloth, or a salted fish for an apple.

Instead, some of the buyers waved their hands in some kind of magical alchemy she could not discern. Others, however, tendered slim silvery cards that seemed to serve as currency. Puzzlingly, the shopkeeper girls always handed the cards back at the end of the transaction.

Descending, Brea tried to catch a clearer view of the card.

"Brr." One of the shop girls pulled her sweater more tightly about her shoulders. "Can you believe management has the air on at this time of year?"

"I don't feel anything," her nearest companion said.

Realizing her presence was being sensed, Brea veered away, rising once more to the bright rows of lights.

A flicker of light and sound beckoned her attention to the far wall where a row of framed images were displayed. Yet these were not motionless portraits, but living depictions, seeming so real she might drift into the very picture and be transported to a different place. What strange human magic was this?

One screen showed an earnest young man leaping through the trees, pursued by fierce wild creatures. Another showed a beautiful woman declaring her love for a bored-looking fellow dressed all in black, while a third featured a disembodied voice describing a scene full of rubble and smoke.

A bright flicker of color made her turn and watch, bemused, as a chipper girl extolled the virtues of a cream one could apply to hands and face. That seemed to end quickly, and another woman appeared, holding up a glass of green liquid called SupaVitaWata, and drinking deeply. Then a boy floating above the ground on something termed a *g-board*.

It was overwhelming, yet she could not tear herself away. Information washed over her like waves, each one bearing some new thought or product or emotion, until she was waterlogged.

She soon understood that in order to function as a human in this new world she would need a number of *devices*. A tablet, or two, or three. A messager. A card that held credits upon it. Another that identified her.

The last two could be replaced by something called a wrist chip, but that seemed an enchantment beyond her means. It would be simpler to conjure up cards than to try to work out the intricacies of imbedding the information into her skin.

She was about to turn away when a feature flashed upon the nearest screen. It showed a large collection of youths attending a sporting event. Attention sharpening, she concentrated on the image, ignoring the uniformed players running about the green field in favor of observing the crowd.

This! This was what she sought. A concentration of people young enough to be susceptible to the mark of magic, yet old enough to be able to move about the world without a chaperone.

Using her magic, she nudged that screen's volume up until she could hear.

"...and once again a disappointing night for Crestview

High, as the Cougars lose their third straight game of the season."

Now she noticed the large letters inscribed at the edge of the field, spelling out *Crestview High School*.

Once she obtained the items she needed for her existence in the human world, she had a new goal. Whatever a high school might be, she would discover how to enter it and become a student there. It was the perfect place to carry out the Dark Queen's mission.

Hours later, bewildered and bedazzled from spending so much time in front of the screens, Brea floated beneath the orange-washed clouds obscuring the night sky and let the breeze bear her back to her shelter.

The stained floor and broken windows made it seem a hovel compared to the riches she had just seen. Yet it was *her* hovel. And unlike the glass palaces of the shops, here she could feel the wind as it blew in through the half-collapsed roof. The stars, when they shone, were visible overhead, and the rain and dew could enter as they willed.

Wearily, she let herself become solid flesh. She had over-taxed herself. After staggering to fetch a cup of water, she curled up in the middle of the floor, but sleep eluded her. Instead, hyper-colored visions flashed through her mind, a montage of everything she had seen upon the screens.

Tomorrow, she must set about establishing herself in the mortal world. At least she knew where to begin—with gear and clothing and a reconnaissance of the place called Crestview High...

Sleep overtook her like a fast-moving hawk, catching her

up in its claws all unawares. When Brea next blinked, morning light lay sluggish across the floor, mirroring her own state.

Sighing, she fetched water, then stepped outside. The dead tree beside her sagging doorway rustled, as if in sympathy. She was tempted to nurture it, to pour her magical energy into its restoration—and in another time and place, she would have.

But the queen's geas lay heavy upon her. There would be no squandering her small store of magic simply to rescue one tree.

Sipping from her broken cup, she let the pale sunshine warm her cheeks. Today, she would be herself. Not quite fey. Not quite mortal—but close enough to pass for one.

A temporary glamour would give her suitable clothing while she visited the palatial stores. As for the card full of credits, a quick act of duplicate conjury should do. Finesse the details with a nudge of magic, and she would be able to purchase whatever she needed.

Transporting everything might prove more difficult, but sometimes plain effort was the better choice. She could conserve her energy if she hand-carried her purchases back into the Exe. Of course a touch of concealment would be in order, but that was far easier than trying to magically transport items from one place to another.

A breath of wind, a shimmer of light, and a hidden alleyway later, she emerged on the street full of shops. Cautiously, she shot glances at her reflection in the windows as she passed.

Her dark hair held a sheen of silver, which she quickly muted. For her illusion, she wore the type of trousers called *jeans*, and a gray sweater that matched the color of her eyes. Her skin was pale, but not remarkably so. She appeared to be a normal girl, of an age termed a *teenager* in the modern world.

Holding her head high in an attempt to look as though she belonged, Brea entered the enormous shop she had explored the day before. Her first task was to mirror-magic one of the cards so that she could procure the items she desired.

Under the guise of perusing a display of handbags, she sidled close to the purchasing area. When the next customer handed her card to the shop girl, Brea closed her eyes in concentration and hummed beneath her breath. A moment later, a silvery card appeared in her hand. Fortunately, it was not made of metal but of the material the mortals called plastic, which seemed to be everywhere.

Brea tapped her index finger three times upon the card, imbuing it with endless credits, the name *Brea Cairgead*, and the attribute of unquestioning acceptance. The effort left her a tiny bit dizzy. She would need to stock up on bottles of water to carry with her for replenishment.

"Are you all right, miss?" A man wearing the uniform of store security paused beside her. Concern and suspicion mixed in equal parts in his expression.

"I am well." She made sure to flash the card at him. "Just a trifle hungry."

"Gotta watch that low blood sugar." He nodded knowingly. "Restaurant three doors down."

"My thanks." The word tripped on her tongue, but he didn't seem to notice. In the Realm of Faerie, one did not bestow thanks, for it was an obligation and an unwelcome debt laid upon the recipient.

Yet it was customary in the human world, and her mission was to become as human-seeming as possible. Affixing a smile to her face, Brea went outside, aware that the guard watched her depart. It was for the best to test the card away from his suspicious gaze, in case her magics had gone awry.

The small café down the block was a tranquil haven, paneled in dark wood with actual, living plants decorating the wide windowsills and a tiny fountain playing near the door. She let out a sigh, then hovered awkwardly, unsure of the protocol.

"Go ahead and take a seat anywhere," the serving girl said, waving one hand.

Brea chose a table beside the window, where the airy brush of ferns against her arm steadied her even further. It was frightening, being out in the world and interacting with mortals. She half-expected them to point and scream, decrying her as inhuman and then doing something barbaric, like tying her to a stake to be burned alive.

She shuddered at the thought of such a hideous fate and attempted to distract herself by reading one of the colorful menus stacked upon the table.

"Herbal tea and a bowl of soup, please," she said when the bespectacled serving girl came to inquire.

The tea would be lovely, and she would pretend to eat the soup. She would take no mortal food, only pure liquids infused with flowers and leaves. Indeed, when the soup arrived, the scent of it made her feel ill. It would provide excuse enough for her to linger, however, so she pushed the bowl to the side and concentrated on the steam wafting up from her tea.

Spearmint and chamomile, which grew in the meadows on the brighter edges of the Dusk Vale. The scent made a wave of longing rush through her. Would she ever return again to the stream she called home, or leap and splash in the silvery waters of the nearby lake?

Such thoughts had no profit to them, and she resolutely turned her mind away.

And if there was an echo of loneliness to the idea of returning to her existence in the vale, what of it? She was a solitary fey, needing no companionship except the dragonflies to dance with and the ripples of wind on the water to sing her to sleep.

"Anything else?" the serving girl asked as she passed Brea's table.

Brea shook her head and handed the girl the silver card, willing her fingers not to tremble. If the worst happened, klaxons sounded and guards appeared, she could always disappear into a mist and float away.

Trying not to appear obvious, she watched the serving girl swipe the card. Nothing dire occurred, and Brea let out a tiny, relieved sigh.

"Thanks for coming in!" the girl said, returning her card and a printout.

"My pleasure." Brea rose, then hesitated.

From the dozens of vids she had absorbed the night before, she understood it was customary to leave a token of thanks at the table.

With a thought, she conjured up a few coins and nudged them next to the plate. She hoped they would not turn to leaves the next morning, in the way of faerie gold. But since she had no actual money, the deception couldn't be helped.

Confidence quickening her stride, Brea went back into the glass palace of wonders and proceeded to purchase everything she found both beautiful and useful. A velvet coverlet the color of sapphire-blue water, a set of pure crystal drinking goblets, a small chest with bronze fittings, two pillows filled with goose-down, and, more for fancy than practicality, a string of colorful glass baubles to hang from one of the broken-out windows.

Her cart was full—overfull—and she had not begun to select her wardrobe. It would be difficult enough to carry this much back to her hideout in the Exe, so she made herself stop. Only then was she aware of the weariness pulsing through her.

The lights overhead seemed suddenly far too bright, searing her eyes, and she wanted to curl up on one of the display beds and sleep.

Instead, she scraped up the strength to finish making her purchases, then lugged the bulky bags out of the shop.

Back on the sidewalk, the hum of metal assailed her. More vehicles traveled the street now, and her reserves had fallen too low. Oh, curses upon her small store of strength, so quickly depleted! She staggered to the end of the block and halted, her chest rising and falling with the beginnings of panic.

No, she would not crumble and weep. Had she not already proved she was strong enough to face the human world? She must simply be more clever.

Tipping her face to the sky, she hummed a rhyme of lightness, of ease, and the bags she carried lifted, each one weighing no more than a vial of moon dust, a spiral of silk.

Exhaustion pulled at her, but she made herself walk sure and straight down the streets until she reached the squalid alleyways bordering the Exe.

Then, with the last droplets of her strength, she tugged a concealing enchantment over herself. By the time she gained the safety of her shelter, she was weaving and stumbling like the town drunk.

Nearly weeping with relief, Brea dragged herself over the threshold and set her bags on the floor. Her wards of protection emitted a serene silver glow, showing that no one had breached the boundary while she was away. It was all she could do to pull the coverlet out of its bag and wrap herself in it before she plummeted into exhausted sleep.

The sun chased the moon across the sky four times before Brea awoke fully. She lay upon the floor, reveling in the softness of azure velvet pulled up around her chin, and stared at the evening-shrouded sky visible through her half-broken roof. A strange feeling washed through her, different from the simple acceptance of things she felt when in her waterbound form. If she had to name it, she might call it *contentment*.

Ah, it was dangerous, to feel such things as a mortal again. She must harden herself, for she could not afford any more weaknesses.

As shadows stole into the room, she fetched her customary cup of water, drinking from the delicate edge of one of her new goblets. She cast a small golden ball of light for illumination while she unpacked the bags, hung her sun catcher in the window, then pulled out the bronze-bound chest.

She let three drops of water run off her fingers, each one imbuing an enchantment into the wood: protection, concealment, safekeeping. Carefully, she placed the medallion into the chest, then closed it and murmured a word of binding. Blue lines flared, and the magic was set.

The chest went into the corner, her new bedding pulled beneath the intact portion of the roof, her set of goblets arrayed in the bathing room. It was a start, and a good one at that.

Now she must attire herself with human clothing and, even more essential, purchase at least one screen device, that center of the much-changed mortal world.

As she had done before, Brea floated to the area where the shops were, then transformed herself into human form. She entered a shop with garments on display, and soon discovered the immense frustration of having to find clothes of the proper size and shape.

Cloaking herself in starlight and mist was so much simpler! Illusions did not tug or squeeze or hang imperfectly upon her form the way physical clothing did. It took the better part of the day just to assemble a few outfits, when she had envisioned being able to complete her entire wardrobe in a few simple hours.

Unlike the first time she had attempted to shop, she monitored her energy levels. When tiredness began to tug upon her bones, Brea completed her purchases and took them back to her shelter.

She did the same the next day, and the next, and her possessions grew: clothing of all kinds, jewelry, a small store of cosmetics, scavenged boxes to keep her new belongings in, and an increasing collection of tablet devices.

She found herself fascinated by them—those small flat screens holding such power and magic. The Brea of her past would have thought such things darkest sorcery, and indeed both the mortal and fae parts of herself were dazzled and a little frightened by the technology. *Tech*, as the humans called it.

It was beginning to make sense, how the simulation game called Feyland had intersected with the Realm of Faerie. One type of magic meeting another, in a place that was neither real nor unreal, and anything was possible. No wonder the Dark Queen was determined to pull as many mortals as she could into her dying Realm. Their dreams, their sorrows, their blood would revitalize the land.

Brea shivered at what that ultimately meant to the humans and their world. But despite her qualms, she was bound to do the queen's bidding.

Still, she delayed. Before she embarked upon her mission, she must find one more pair of soft leather boots, and an amulet made of amber to match the bracelet she had procured the other day. New tablets were announced, and surely she could not begin her work for the queen until she was outfitted with the newest devices.

She had been in the mortal world a fortnight, and that first, warm kernel of contentment was beginning to grow into something more. A sensation she had all but forgotten. Happiness.

Perhaps you might simply stay here, a small, treacherous part of herself whispered. *Do not return to the Realm, do not put your touch upon the humans. Just make this tiny, perfect life for yourself.*

It was tempting, and yet she knew it would never succeed. Beyond the fact that some nights loneliness still shrouded her in a cold fog, the Dark Queen would not turn a blind eye to Brea shirking her duties.

She had been sent to the human world to make youths susceptible to the magic of the Realm, so that when they played Feyland they would slip and tumble into the queen's clutches instead of staying safely within the confines of the game. Here, in the city of Crestview, mortals had already crossed that boundary more than once, making it more permeable and easier to bend to the Dark Queen's wishes.

Brea was but a tool in the queen's implacable hand.

The next morning she awoke with the aftermath of frightening dreams still shivering through her. Redcap goblins had chased her through the Exe, the queen had stared at her until she had felt a blackthorn dart through her heart. Clutching her chest, Brea had felt hot blood flow through her fingers.

The warnings were clear. She must not delay any further.

Brea flicked on her newest tablet and typed out the words of her next, inevitable step. *How to become a high school student.*

Twenty minutes later, with a touch of enchantment humming inside the system, she had an identity as an exchange student from Ireland staying with a fictitious host family. With a last tap upon the screen, the deed was done. She was now enrolled as a junior at Crestview High—and expected to begin classes the very next Monday. Fear shivered through her at the thought.

But had she not used her wits and small magic to succeed among the mortals? As daunting as this next part of her mission might be, she would face it and show the Dark Court that she was not a helpless creature to be gutted and tossed aside.

She was a faerie girl. Whether the human world knew it or not, she would put her mark upon it—silvery and magical, shining with the light of a hundred invisible stars.

⚘

Author's Note: *Brea's Tale* falls between *Spark* and *Royal* in the Feyland series. Haven't started this award-winning, *USA Today* bestselling series yet? *The First Adventure,* the prequel novella, is FREE at all retailers!

Thank you to Samuel Peralta and the Future Chronicles, where portions of this novella first appeared. As always, thanks to my fabulous editor, Laurie, for knowing the world of Feyland so well and keeping me on track.

THE FAERIE INVASION

RIC GARCIA RAN, breath scraping his throat as his over-full backpack slammed his spine. Behind him, the heavy tread of his pursuer shook the rubbled streets.

Two months ago, he would have laughed at the thought of being chased by an ogre down Vista's main street. That kind of stuff belonged in sim games or fantasy books, not real life.

But that was before the invasion.

He dodged around a squat, stucco building and forced his legs to pump out more speed. Just a little farther. His iron crowbar might hurt the twenty feet of enraged ogre chasing him, but ultimately he was going to be lunch.

Good thing the crowbar had other uses than defending against the fey folk.

Ric skidded to a stop halfway down the block, in front of a round sewer grate. He forced the tip of the crowbar under the grate and heaved. Dammit! The heavy metal didn't budge.

The ogre rounded the corner. A hideous smile stretched its mouth wide, showing blackened teeth as it reached for its cudgel.

"I see you, youngling. Tender eating, yes."

Desperately, Ric threw all his weight against the bar. With a rusty squeal, the grating lifted. He pivoted, scraping the grate over the pavement until the opening was big enough for him to slip through. He hoped.

The ogre was close enough to smell now, the stench of rancid meat and old sweat wafting down the street. Ric flung himself down and got his legs into the hole, then his hips. Crap, the backpack. No way was it going to fit.

He tore it off and shoved it to the side, hoping the ogre wouldn't crush it under those huge, flat feet. Ric's scavenging had yielded treasure, but his life was even more important.

"Come back, morsel!" the ogre cried, lumbering into a run once more.

Ric's feet found the ladder on the side of the pipe. He forced his shoulders past the grate, feeling his T-shirt tear and his skin burn. Hopefully there wouldn't be much blood. Goblins could smell it, and track him that way.

He ducked low and began scrambling down the ladder. Overhead, his pursuer flung the sewer grate away as if were a penny. The light faded as the ogre reached into the hole. Thankfully, it couldn't jam its thick hand into the opening, but had to resort to sticking a couple fingers in. One brushed the top of Ric's head and his foot slipped as he pushed himself faster.

He scrabbled at the rungs, caught his balance, then went down a few more feet before he let himself stop. Hooking one elbow through the rung, he hung there, panting. The ogre raged and stomped around above him, but the creature was too dumb to wait for him to emerge. Some unlucky soul would divert its attention and it would leave, forgetting about Ric.

A trickle of liquid sounded from somewhere below the

soles of his battered Converse. Just a trickle, not a rushing stream. There weren't that many people left to run the water in their kitchen sinks, or flush their toilets.

Everything was breaking down. Because of the Faerie Invasion.

It sounded so ridiculous. And at first the invasion had only been a little freaky, and a little comical. Water sprites in the drinking fountain at school. Pixies flying around at night, causing traffic accidents.

News reporters said the world governments were "handling" the sudden influx of magical creatures. Stay calm. Nothing to worry about.

Then the mer-folk had swamped New York, the sea-witches had drowned Los Angeles, and most of the broadcasts had stopped.

After that, things had gotten severe pretty quickly. Mortals had learned to stay inside after dark, when the Wild Hunt rode, harvesting souls and sowing madness in their wake. Old lore was rediscovered, and people started carrying iron with them. Before the 'net went down, the main sites were flooded with information about how to repel the fey folk.

Cold iron was one of the best ways, and apparently people broke into museums to steal the armor and swords. Unfortunately, Vista was just a podunk town with only the Museum of Hispanic Art. Ric couldn't see himself fighting off ogres and goblins by brandishing a painting or clay pot.

Salt sprinkled across thresholds and windowsills was supposed to help. Unless the fey folk could dislodge it with wind or water, and then come right into your house.

Supposedly the creatures could be held at bay with various herbs and charms. Too bad they were made of things that didn't grow around Vista, or stuff Ric wouldn't recognize if he saw it.

Going to the supermarket for supplies was too dangerous now. The faeries had figured out pretty quick that humans needed food, and stores were their favorite hunting grounds.

Sure, there were a few crazies that had walked out with open arms, begging the fey folk to take them. Some had been messily eaten. Some had just disappeared.

It was mostly horrible, and Ric was worried the human race was going down. Although, a few times he'd experienced breathtaking things: a beautiful maiden with gossamer wings floating in the moonlight, a strand of melody so sweet he thought his heart would break, a glowing ring of mushrooms in the park, where creatures danced and glimmered.

By the time the ogre stomped off, Ric's heartbeat had calmed to normal. Still, he waited a good fifteen minutes, just to be sure. No way was he leading that thing back to his little sister.

Angelina was probably worried by now. But she was a smart kid, and knew how to lay low in the hiding place they'd found. They'd be okay.

Nothing's ever going to be okay again, his conscience whispered.

Shut up, he said back.

The Garcia family would make it, the way they always had. From wars in Mexico to illegal immigration to full status as U.S. citizens. Some storybook creatures weren't going to take them out. He knew that wherever the rest of his family had ended up—Mama, Papa, Aunt Dolores and his annoying cousins—they were fighters.

Even Angelina was going to get better. His pack was full of medicines from the pharmacy he'd looted. Something in there would help her, would stop her from coughing all the time, and restore her appetite.

Carefully, he emerged from the sewer, the late sunlight elongating his shadow as he crept to the curb. Ric fished in his pocket and pulled out the red knit hat his aunt had made him last year. He jammed it on his head, then grabbed his backpack —thankfully untrampled—and slung it over his shoulders. Then he bent over, cocked one shoulder up, and let his other arm hang down to his knees.

Up close, he was clearly a human, but at a distance he could be mistaken for a redcap goblin. Unless he ran into another ogre, who could smell a human from twenty yards away.

He shambled down the street, taking his time. Down one side street he glimpsed the twiggy forms of spriggans, but they were going the other direction. He skirted the shops where the pixies had taken up residence. They were easy to avoid, the windows glowing with pale silver light.

He stayed away from the residential areas all together. Too depressing, and in some cases, gruesome. Instead, he headed down to Vista's industrial sector.

At the end of the main street, he stopped and glanced over his shoulder. Nothing seemed to be following him. Still lurching, he turned down Coronado Way. The warehouses rising around him were untouched—nothing of interest there for the fey folk.

He picked up his pace, scuttling forward until he came to the boarded-up window covered by bent metal bars. It had taken a lot of prying for him to fit, although Angelina had slipped through, no problem. She'd laughed at him, her dark eyes flashing, calling him *gordo*.

Any extra weight he might've carried was long gone, though. Both of them were getting too thin—especially

Angelina. Even though he generally found enough things for them to eat, she was growing more and more listless. Some days he had to spoon-feed her.

But the medicines in his pack would help. They had to.

He rapped out their secret code on the plywood. After a few moments the board scraped aside, just enough for his sister to peep out.

"*¿Quien es?*" she asked.

"*Soy yo,*" he answered.

They figured the fey folk wouldn't know Spanish. For whatever reason, all the creatures came from British Isles fairy tales and lore. *La Llorona* and the other ghosts and demons from their own tradition seemed to be missing from the invasion. So far.

Angelina gave him a weak smile and pushed the board wider.

"Took you long enough," she said, for a minute sounding like a nine-year-old version of Mama.

"I ran into complications."

He climbed through the bars and into the boxy room they'd claimed as their hiding place. Until a few weeks ago, it had been an office for some warehouse manager. On the opposite wall was a metal door with a wire-webbed window, and another, larger window that looked out into the shadowy cavern of the abandoned warehouse.

They'd covered that window with dark blankets, and put a blackout curtain over the one on the door. The room was plenty big enough for their sleeping pallet, their clothes and few possessions, and their makeshift kitchen: hotplate, microwave, small fridge, and electric kettle, plus assorted dishes and pots.

So far the electricity had stayed on, though a couple times

it had flickered wildly. Every time, Ric's heart squeezed tight. Already parts of the town were dead. He didn't like to think about what would happen when the lights finally gave out.

He pulled the board back over the window and set the two-by-four across that held it in place. The room dimmed, and he clicked on the desk lamp they'd found in the office. The illumination made Angelina's cheekbones stand out from the hollows of her cheeks, and he tried to tell himself it was just a trick of the light.

"So?" She set her hands on her hips. "What did you get?"

He shrugged the heavy pack off.

"I got some medicine to make you feel better, *hermanita*." He pulled the plastic bottles out and lined them up on the cement floor.

She made a face. "I don't like pills."

"I know. But I also found these." He held up the three chocolate bars, and her eyes brightened. "And one more thing."

He unzipped the side pocket of the backpack and drew out the best treasure yet.

"Oranges!" Angelina stuck out her thin hand, and he placed one in her palm, trying not to notice how her fingers trembled.

So far, the fey folk hadn't learned to stake out the gas-station convenience stores. They probably had at first, but nobody drove now. Talk about making yourself an obvious target. The store Ric had plundered that afternoon still had a decent stock of snack food. And fruit by the abandoned registers. The bananas had turned to blackened slime, and the apples were all mushy, but the oranges were still good.

The sharp smell of citrus filled the room as Angelina ripped hers open. Mouth watering, he did the same. They sat without talking for a few minutes, a neat pile of orange rind on the floor between them while they savored the treat.

"Don't lick your fingers," he said, when they were finished.

"But it tastes so good."

"And you'll be sticky all night. Come on, wash up."

He dampened one of the dishtowels they'd scavenged. So far, water wasn't an issue, although he'd give almost anything for a hot shower. Sponge baths were getting old.

Angelina let him clean her face off, too, then yawned.

"Bedtime, sleepyhead," he said. "And take a couple pills."

He tapped an antibiotic and a few vitamins out into his palm and handed them to his sister. She obediently swallowed them with a few sips of water, made a dreadful face, then crawled to her side of the pallet without argument.

They both were sleeping a lot. He didn't know if was because they were getting malnourished, or the stress of having to hide all the time.

Sure, they were alive, but it wasn't the greatest life. Angelina hardly got to play at all now, and his days were long swaths of boredom punctuated by moments of extreme panic. The adventure of surviving had gotten old pretty quick.

But he didn't know what else they could possibly do. There was nowhere to go. This wasn't one of those happy stories where a brave enclave of humans holed up in the hills battled off the invaders, and emerged to restore the world.

Ric tucked Angelina's fuzzy pink blanket over her. Good thing they lived in a warm climate. Winter was going to be chilly, but they wouldn't freeze to death.

If they made it to winter.

As his sister's quiet breathing deepened into sleep, Ric rolled over and grabbed one of the books he'd borrowed from the library. It wasn't stealing if there was nobody left to check books out, right?

The shelf of folktales and fairy lore had been partially

ransacked by the time he thought of it, but there were still enough books left to take an armful and leave some for the next person. So far, though, he hadn't found any answers about how to stop a faerie invasion.

From what he'd been able to gather before he and Angelina had gone into hiding, somehow a gateway had opened between the human world and the Realm of Faerie. The president and world leaders were planning to negotiate with the king and queen of the Realm, but clearly they hadn't gotten very far before things broke down entirely.

Outside, a long howl shivered through the night. Ric cocked his head, listening. The thunder of spectral horses galloping through the sky, the winding cry of a hunting horn, the shrill yapping of red-eyed hounds drifting through the air. . .

The Wild Hunt was riding.

He snapped off the light. Early on in the invasion, he'd glimpsed the hunt out his bedroom window. The memory still made him shudder—especially the sight of the leader of the hunt, a dark figure with huge antlers silhouetted against the eerily-lit sky.

In the darkness, Ric set the book aside, then kicked off his shoes and pulled another blanket over himself. Not that he'd be able to get to sleep while the night echoed with creepy sounds, but there was nothing else to do.

Still, he must have dozed, because the sound of something scratching at the board covering the window brought him wide-awake. After a moment, the light pawing turned to wood ripping under claws, accompanied by a snuffling and grunts of anticipation.

Ice swept over him.

They'd been discovered.

Beside him, he felt Angelina go rigid. She must be awake and hearing the noise, too. He reached his hand over and felt for hers, then gave it a tight squeeze. The sound of shredding plywood intensified.

Ric slipped his hand free and groped for the crowbar. If this was it, he'd go down fighting.

A hound bayed right outside, the sound jarring through him like a physical blow. Angelina whimpered as he stood up, and he wished her could reassure her—but they both knew the situation was dire.

The cement floor was cold under his bare feet. But not as cold as his heart as he faced the boarded-up window.

With a crack, the plywood fell into three pieces. A sinuous, ghostly hound slithered through the opening in the bars, skinny enough to pass through without touching the iron. It landed on the cement, eyes shining with red light, and growled.

"Stay back." Ric brandished his crowbar.

A hollow laugh boomed through the room, and outside, the antlered leader of the hunt held up his hand. He was surrounded by a dozen elfin knights on shadowy steeds. Their faces were beautiful and terrible to gaze upon, their long, silver hair shining like moonlight.

"So brave, you mortals, always," the huntsman said. "And so foolish. Come out."

"I don't think so." Ric swiped at the hound, but the creature dodged back.

Another one slipped through the window, then another. An eerie glow illuminated the room, and Ric shot a look at his sister. There was no way they were going to make it through this alive. Her dark hair was tangled with sleep, her eyes wide with fear in her gaunt face.

"I love you, Angel," he said, his throat tight. "Always and forever."

Ahh. A sigh swept over the riders outside, and their radiance increased, as though someone had turned up a dimmer knob.

"Come out," the antlered figure said. "Or would you prefer to be rent by the teeth of my hounds?"

The nearest one growled, its red eyes glowing.

"Why, so you can chase us down again?" Ric poked the crowbar at the hound, and it skittered away.

"No. We are charged with taking you to our queen."

Ric hesitated. He'd be an idiot not to take the chance. But everything he'd read about faerie bargains only showed the fey folk were not to be trusted.

"Let's go outside," Angelina whispered. "I don't want to be bitten to death."

"Okay." Ric raised his voice so the huntsman could hear him. "Call off your dogs. We'll come."

"Leave your cold iron behind," the huntsman replied.

Fair enough, though Ric waited until the last hound slunk through the barred window before setting his crowbar down. It clanked against the floor, a forlorn sound. The sound of safety, being abandoned. Not like they had a choice, though. Not really.

Angelina stood up, clutching the thin blanket around her shoulders. She looked more wraithlike than ever in the eerie light.

"Keep your blanket," Ric told her, eyeing the horses and riders.

Wherever the Wild Hunt was taking them, a little protection from the elements couldn't hurt. He snagged his black hoodie and shrugged it on, then climbed out the window.

Turning, he helped Angelina out, then held her hand as they faced the awful beauty of the Wild Hunt. One of the riders urged his mount forward, heatless flames flickering around its hooves. Ric's heart gave a thump of terror, but he stood his ground.

"I will carry the little one," the faerie said, his voice like ice crystals chiming together.

Angelina stared up at the elfin knight, awe filling her thin face.

"You better take us to the same place," Ric said, like he was in a position to make demands.

"Have no fear," the knight said. "All roads lead to the Dark Court."

He gestured with one long-fingered hand, and Angelina rose gently into the air. She gave a small gasp, then smiled at Ric as she floated up to the rider's saddle.

"I'm flying," she said.

Ric blinked fast, clearing the hot tears from his eyes. He had to be strong for his little sister. And himself. He had to stop counting her smiles as if each one were the last he'd ever see.

"Be gentle with her," he said, giving the knight a hard stare.

The faerie only regarded him, centuries fathom-deep in his eyes, until Ric had to look away.

"Have you courage enough to ride with me?" the antlered leader of the hunt asked.

"Why not?" Ric tried to sound casual, despite the fear clogging his throat.

One second he was standing on the rutted pavement, the next, invisible bonds snaked about his chest, pinning his arms tight as he was tugged into the air. He did his best not to yelp, especially as Angelina was watching him.

Instead of drifting gently to land in the front of the saddle, the way his sister had, Ric was roughly deposited on the back of the horse, behind the huntsman. He started slipping off, and the rider reached back with a hand as hard as stone and hauled him back.

"You must hold fast to me," the huntsman said, an echo of deep laughter shading his voice.

Great. Ric supposed it was too late to change his mind. Besides, he was brave enough for this. Really he was.

Clenching his jaw, he grabbed hold of the rider's waist. It was like holding on to an unyielding statue, nothing alive there at all, but Ric made himself hang on.

The huntsman raised one gloved hand, then snapped it down. Instantly, the horn sounded and the horses leaped into the sky. Cold wind whipped Ric's hair and made his eyes water. The hounds yapped fiercely, swirling about the fiery hooves. A sickle moon shone high above the riders, and from somewhere Ric heard the cry and wail of bagpipes.

Below them, the orange streetlights of Vista shrank, ranked in their orderly rows. More than half the city was black, though, and as Ric watched, several blocks of the city went dark.

Then they were speeding over rocky, shrub-dotted hills, gaining altitude until he could see the very edge of the ocean shining to the west.

Something swirled in the air in front of them, half-glimpsed around the huntsman's broad shoulders. Blue fire outlined what could only be a gateway back into the Realm of Faerie. The first hounds reached it, and winked out, and Ric braced himself.

Maybe he screamed—he wasn't sure. All he knew was that every cell of his body felt like it had been dipped in liquid flame. Breathing harshly though his nose, he forced back the taste of orange-flavored bile at the back of his throat.

It took a few minutes to feel like he was all there. He was surprised he hadn't let go and fallen off the fey horse, but somehow his arms still clung to the huntsman's waist. Despite the wind tearing at his breath, he turned his head to make sure Angelina was okay.

The rider bearing her was close behind. She sat upright in the saddle, seemingly unhurt, though her face was pale.

"You all right?" he yelled, the words snatched from his lips by the cold air.

She stuck one hand out of the fuzzy pink blanket and gave him a thumbs up.

Ric closed his eyes for a moment. He couldn't believe this was really happening—but then, life had been a nightmare for the past several weeks. Why not make it worse?

When he opened his eyes again, his breath caught at the view. Stars sparkled overhead, a thousand times brighter than in the human world, each one a laser beam of pure white light. The crescent moon was still there, but it spilled moonlight like water over the fantastical land below.

Groves of tall, pale-barked trees danced, their silver leaves flashing. At the top of a hill stood a circle of standing stones, shining with inscribed runes. Beyond the circle lay an orchard filled with gemlike fruit, a golden apple glowing in the highest tree.

The smell of sweet flowers drifted up as they rode over a field of pale blossoms. The sound of pipes were now joined by a flute and drum, weaving a melody both happy and sad. Giants shambled over the distant meadows, and mysterious lights beckoned from the marshlands.

This was the Realm of Faerie.

Despite himself, the enchantment of it filled Ric's senses. No matter how horrible the fey folk were, and how overrun his own world, this was magic, and part of his soul yearned for it. Had yearned for it his whole life.

The riders began to drift lower in the sky, heading for the dark woods ahead. Gnarled branches of ancient oak trees rose into the night, surrounding a clearing in the center of the forest. As they rode closer, Ric could see a bonfire flickering there, eerie purple flames illuminating long feasting tables and a throng of fey folk.

The far side of the clearing glowed with pale blue light. A throne made of tangled vines rose over the gathering, and upon that throne sat the most beautiful woman Ric had ever seen.

Of course, she wasn't really a woman, but a faerie. He knew that, but still couldn't take his gaze from her as the Wild Hunt landed in the clearing.

That must be the Dark Queen.

The huntsman dismounted, then grabbed Ric's arm and pulled him from the back of the fey mount. He managed to keep his feet, and pulled out of the rider's hard grasp. One thing could distract him from the queen: his little sister. He hurried to Angelina's side.

As before, the knight had gently floated her to the ground. Despite that care, she doubled over in a racking cough. Ric slipped his arm around her shoulders, holding her while her body shuddered.

Finally she straightened. The pink blanket was spattered with blood, but her eyes shone with wonder.

"Hang in there," he said.

His heart wrenched at how pale her face was. Riding through the shivering wind and going through the gateway surely had overtaxed her already weak system. She looked worse than ever, her skin practically translucent, almost revealing the bones underneath her flesh.

"Look at this." Her voice came out barely louder than a whisper as she glanced around the clearing. "It's incredible!"

And freaky. Oddly-jointed creatures danced and shambled around the bonfire. Red cap goblins tore at a haunch of meat with their sharp claws. A pale woman with tears of blood falling down her face crooned a lullaby while playing a harp made of bone.

In the shadows, other musicians played, including a man holding a guitar who looked almost human. Near the throne, a small figure sat upon a red and white-speckled toadstool. His hair was full of leaves, his clothing tatters and feathers. Meeting Ric's gaze, he cocked his head and gave a bright-eyed wink.

Three faerie handmaidens hovered behind the queen's throne, their gossamer wings slowly moving back and forth. White moths wove among the dark branches of the trees, like fluttering stars. The air smelled of frost and roses.

"Welcome to my court, mortals," the queen said. "Come pay me your regards."

She beckoned with one long-nailed hand, and the look in her midnight eyes sent a shiver coursing through Ric. Keeping his arm around Angelina's frail shoulders, they walked the few paces to where the queen sat.

"Kneel," the huntsman said.

Ric didn't particularly want to, but the word carried the weight of command. His knees bent, and he and Angelina ended up kneeling on the velvety-soft moss before the throne. At least his sister didn't have to keep standing. Ric slipped his arm down to take her fingers, her hand cold and delicate in his. He held it lightly, afraid of breaking her.

The queen leaned forward, regarding them. Her black hair framed her face, and her gown swirled about her as though made of smoke and stitched together with spiderwebs and starlight.

"What do you want from us?" Ric asked. His mouth was dry with fear, with awe.

"Your dreams," the queen said.

"Really?" He didn't bother keeping the sarcasm from his voice. "You sure you don't want to, like, sacrifice us at the full moon or something?"

She frowned, and clouds rolled over the sky, obscuring the bright stars.

"There has been bloodshed enough," she said, her voice crackling with disapproval. "Indeed, there are almost too few humans left for our purposes. The denizens of the Realm indulged too freely of their own appetites, once given access to your world."

"Maybe you should have stopped them."

Her eyes narrowed, and frost settled on the nearby branches. "Do not tell me how to rule my court, youngling."

Clearly Ric had hit a nerve. He almost pursued it, but despite her talk of too much death, he suspected the queen wouldn't hesitate to turn him into a pile of ashes if he pissed her off any more. Already he could tell he was riding the line.

He gently squeezed Angelina's hand. No way was he letting anything happen to her. *Hah*—like he had a choice.

"What do you mean, your purposes?" he asked.

"The Realm of Faerie requires the essence of mortality to remain in existence," she said.

"Seems like you've taken a lot of that, already." He had no

idea how many hundreds of thousands of people had died, but it was a ton.

"It is not the *deaths* of humans we need—not unless we capture your life essence in the process which, alas, only too few of my subjects have done. No, it is your dreams and hopes, your music and art, which feed the Realm and sustains us. Without that, we shall fade into the shadows and wither in the wind."

Sounded like the queen had made a tactical error in letting the fey creatures run amok in the human world. He didn't say so, though. Clearly she already knew that, and if he got fried, who would look out for Angelina?

Beside him, his sister shivered, then slowly crumpled to the mossy ground.

"Angelina!" He scooped her up in his arms.

Her eyelids fluttered, then opened and she smiled up weakly at him. He could feel her pulse racing.

"*Te amo . . .*" she whispered.

"No. No, you're not dying on me." He didn't care that tears spilled down his cheeks, or that the fey creatures pressed close, their expressions avid. "Stay with me, Angel. Please."

She drew in a long, shuddering breath.

"Save her!" Ric lifted his gaze to the Dark Queen. "I know you can. Please—save her, and I'll give you anything you want."

The air trembled, as though an invisible current coursed through the clearing. The dark clouds rolled back and the stars shone down, showing the last spark of life in Angelina's eyes.

Beware of faerie bargains, his conscience whispered. But it was too late, and anyway he didn't care. He'd give up everything to save his sister.

"You know not what you ask," the small creature perched on the toadstool said.

"Silence, Puck," the queen said. "Mortal, I accept your offer. In exchange for saving your sister, you will dwell here in the Realm forever, giving us the sustenance of your humanity."

"Okay," Ric said. "Just hurry." Angelina felt so light in his arms, as though her soul was already halfway gone.

"Set her on the ground before you," the queen said.

He didn't want to let go of her, but did as the queen bid.

"I love you, *hermanita*," he said, gently brushing Angelina's hair back from her forehead. He wasn't sure if she could even hear him any more.

The queen drew a long black thorn from her sleeve. Chanting strange, liquid syllables, she inscribed symbols in the air above Angelina. They glowed with violet light, then shimmered down like trailing fireworks to settle on her body.

The bright sparks began seeping *into* her. Ric forced himself not to brush them away. He hoped they weren't hurting her. Soon, his sister's whole form glowed purple.

Then she began to change.

"Hey!" he cried. "What are you doing to her?"

"Saving her," the queen said, her gaze cold and implacable. "Her human form was failing, so I must give her another."

"That's not what we agreed to." He glanced at his sister's now-elongated hands, the shape of her face sharp-edged and almost alien.

"You only asked that I save her," the queen said. "Not that she remain human."

The sprite, Puck, gave him a sorrowful shake of the head.

Ric swallowed his useless protests. There was nothing he could do, except watch as his sister was transformed into a faerie creature. Would she even know him when it was done?

Finally, the glow faded. The queen spoke a single syllable

more, and Angelina slowly sat up. Her gaze met Ric's, and he braced himself.

For a moment, her dark eyes stared blankly into his. Then something flashed in their depths, and she grinned at him. He tried to ignore the fact that her teeth were now pointed.

"Angelina?" he asked.

"Ric! I feel so *good*." She jumped to her feet and gave him a hug.

He didn't quite know how to hold this new, elongated body of hers. Especially when his hands encountered something strange on her back—a soft, feathery touch against his skin.

"What are those?" he asked, though he suspected he knew.

She pivoted, looking over her shoulder. "Oh my God, I have wings!"

Sure enough. Coming out of her back were two gossamer wings, a rainbow sheen of iridescence on them, like an oil slick on water.

"Now you really are an angel," he said, his voice tight with relief. With regret.

She wasn't the same little girl any more, and he had a feeling that slowly her humanity would fade from her, until she was just another faerie maiden serving the Dark Queen. But it was the bargain he had made.

What would be worse, having her die in his arms, or watching her become something other, each day moving further and further from him? He didn't know. It was an impossible choice.

Angelina waved her wings back and forth, and tilted into struggling flight. Some of the watching fey folk tittered, and Puck bounded into the air. He took Angelina's hand and steadied her, then looked at Ric.

"I will bring her to visit you every day," he said in a high, piping voice.

That didn't sound good.

Ric cleared his throat. "Where is she going?"

The queen laughed, the sound like chiming bells, and Ric turned to face her once more.

"She remains in my court," the queen said. "*You* are one about to depart."

He didn't want to leave Angelina—but he didn't really want to stay in the Dark Court, either.

"Depart to where?" he asked.

The queen tilted her sharp chin and beckoned to a figure standing in the shadows. A human walked forward, a young man who looked a few years older than Ric.

"Royal will show you to your new home in the mortal compound," she said. "Every month, at the new moon, expect a summons to court."

"But I'll see my sister every day, right?" he asked, giving her a hard look.

"As Puck has said. Now be gone. I weary of this conversation."

She turned away and one of her handmaidens placed a gem-studded silver goblet in her hand. The music rose, harp and drum and guitar weaving a jaunty melody through the clearing, and most of the watching fey folk returned to their former pastimes. Angelina still hovered lopsidedly in the air, her hand in Puck's.

"Say 'bye to your sister, and let's go," the human called Royal said.

"Is that really your name?" Ric asked.

"Yeah."

Royal didn't explain, just waited as Angelina made an

awkward landing and Ric hugged her again. No matter what she looked like, part of sister was still there, inside. At least for now.

"Enjoy your wings, Angel," he said. "I'll see you tomorrow."

Whatever tomorrow meant in the Realm of Faerie. He hoped it would be soon.

Royal led him out of the clearing and through the moon-gilded oaks, toward the dubious protection of the mortal compound.

Behind him, the glimmer of the Dark Court faded.

Before him, the future stretched into forever, an eternity spent dreaming of the lost and empty human world.

Author's Note: This tale was written for the *Visions of the Apocalypse* anthology, where authors were asked to envision the end of the world. I set this story within my Feyland universe, looking at what might happen if the faeries won. But don't worry - they won't! It was simply an exploration of the idea. An alternate ending in a different universe than our own, perhaps-

GOBLIN IN LOVE

CRIK NOBSHINS RAISED his wooden cup, toasting the latest goblin raid along with the others in his riot. Amid the smacking of lips and yowling laughter, he took a long guzzle of the bitter ale. He didn't relish the flavor, but was desperate to rinse away the slimy taste of raw meat still lingering in his mouth.

"Good fighting today, Crik." Bonewort, the yellow-eyed leader of the riot, clouted him between the shoulders. "Your first outing. We'll make a raider of you yet."

Crik bared his teeth in what he hoped would be taken for a grin rather than a grimace. Violet light from the nearby bonfire flickered over the faces of his claw-mates in the riot, glinted off their slanted eyes and sharp teeth. The gnarled oak trees overhead scraped the starlit sky, and the small clearing pulsed with the thud of drums.

"Aye," he ground out, hoping it was enough.

"We raid again after this slumber." The leader gave him a sly look. "You go as Knocker next time, up front. Need to bloody your cap more."

Crik glanced at Bonewort's cap, which glowed bright red by the fitful light of the fire. His own cap was still a muddy brown, with only a faint scarlet edging. The thought of dipping it into a pool of lesser faerie's blood made his stomach knot.

But he was a redcap goblin, on his way to becoming a full member of Bonewort's riot. Hunting down the weaker fey for sport and meat, then washing their goblin caps in the spilt blood was what redcaps did. That, and the bidding of their mistress, the Dark Queen, who ruled over the midnight part of the Realm.

He didn't know which would be worse—finishing the process of turning his cap bright red, or carrying out the dark tasks the queen demanded of her goblins.

Not that he should find them unpleasant. Redcaps reveled in the chase and the kill, and told gleeful tales of their various bloody exploits while carrying out the court's business. Once, he'd felt the same, but that was before he'd seen *her*, all shining and pure in the watery moonlight.

He nodded to Bonewort. "I'm ready."

"You'd best be." The big goblin gave him a leering grin, then went to join his two Chasers around the fire.

Crik shifted on the bumpy log he'd claimed for his seat, and took another drink of his ale; this time to wash the taste of the lie from between his teeth. He wasn't ready, and he didn't think he'd ever be.

On the night he'd been spawned, one of three in his mother's litter, the goblin wives had gathered around, crooning.

"Ohh, a lad and two girls! Look at the teeth on that one. She'll be a fine fighter."

"And her sister—what lovely orange eyes. You'll be beating the suitors off with a stick."

Crik had a dim memory of his mother's cackle. "She can do it herself."

"A nice nobble to the knees on your boy, too," the neighbor had said. "Fast, he'll be."

The predictions had come true. Crik's first sister was well on the way to becoming lead Chaser in another riot, and his second sister had already whelped a litter of four healthy goblings.

As for himself, he was fast, but completely undistinguished in any other way. Except for the warped streak of sickness that made raw flesh unsavory to him. From an early age, he'd known to hide his disgusting desire for cooked meat, or he'd be next on the prey list.

Sometimes, though, he wondered if that might be a better end than this continual pretense. Choking down gobbets of flesh in public was bad enough, but tonight, the screams of the brownie they'd caught outside the Dusk Vale had made him want to empty his stomach. He'd forced himself to join the circle surrounding the creature, and take his turn at the stabbing. When the brownie died before he could take a second swipe, he'd been sickly grateful.

Bonewort had filled the riot's ceremonial clay bowl with the creature's blood, and Crik had lined up with the rest to dip his cap. For whatever reason—only the one blow, or his youth, or the flaw in his goblin soul—his cap had not turned completely red. Or even half red.

Head down, he'd cast a furtive look at the leader, wondering if he'd revealed himself in some way.

"No sulking," Bonewort had said, noticing his gaze. "Takes more than one blooding to fill a cap."

At least it wasn't a mark of his failings. Yet. But he'd have to keep raiding, keep killing, until his cap turned bright red.

Then what? a small voice whispered inside him. *You'll never be worthy of her, not stinking of blood, with raw meat between your teeth and a cap stained with death.*

And now Bonewort wanted him to take Knocker, be the first to stab and rend.

Hunched over his ale cup, Crik watched the other goblins gnaw the bones of the brownie and cast them into the fire. The lovely smell of scorched flesh reached his nose, and he gulped, forcing himself not to leap up and scrabble through the coals for any last, delicious morsels.

He was a perversion of a goblin, indeed.

When he'd been a young gobling, his second sister had found him sucking the marrow of a cooked bone he'd pulled from the fire.

She'd snatched the bone from his hand. "So hungry you're eating trash? That's disgusting."

Bringing it to her wide slashed nostrils, she'd sniffed, then made a face and flung the tidbit away.

Since then, he'd learned to hide his filthy yearning for cooked flesh. In the thick of the sleeping time, he'd sneak out, stomach growling, to paw through the fire. Always hungry, he'd learned to eat the roots and berries that grew in the dim forests of the Dark Realm. Best of all was a fungus that grew from the sides of the oaks, an orange, chewy mass he'd come to enjoy.

If the other goblins ever found out, they'd turn on him instantly. Weakness wasn't tolerated in the tribe. Either you were a youngling, or a full redcap, or fit only for blood sacrifice.

Just last moon-waxing, one of the old raiders in this very riot had misjudged the teeth of a nixie, and had his leg ripped to shreds. He served now in the Dark Court, waiting for the hour the queen would stab him through the heart with her dagger of black thorn and use his life force to weave her magics.

At least it would be a clean death, unlike what the redcaps would do to Crik if they discovered his perversions. Suppressing a shudder, he set down his empty ale cup and went to roll out his sleeping mat beneath the trees.

Behind his closed eyes, he saw the brownie die, over and over. Although he could feel the edge of joy in it, the rest of him turned away. Beyond his own sickness now was always the thought of *her*, and what she would think of him if she knew he took delight in tormenting creatures weaker than himself.

At last, as the thin moon arced over the trees, Crik rose. He moved quietly away from the last purple embers of the fire, the guttural snores of the riot, and slunk through the forest. On the horizon a faint gray line shone, barely visible unless one knew where to look. He turned his hard-soled feet in that direction.

It was not the first time he'd snuck toward the dusk lands. At least he had the skill of stealth, though he might be lacking in all other redcap qualities. His ability to move quietly had allowed him to observe many of the denizens at the edge of the Dark Realm, and wonder.

How had he come to be born a goblin? Why was his soul not housed in one of the placid brownies, who preferred milk and oat cakes for their meals, or a pixie who ate insects and drank nectar from the blossoms?

When he was a gobling, he'd imagined running away from the night and going to live among the creatures of the Dusk Vale. It had smote his heart, the day he'd stepped from the shadowed trees only to send the nearby fey folk scrambling for safety. Their cries of terror still stung, when he let himself remember.

Crik ripped an orange fungus from a downed log as he passed, swallowing back the memory with each chewy mouthful. Some night, when the moon was just a memory in the sky, he dreamed of showing himself to her. Would he ever screw up the courage? Would he ever be worthy?

The light grew, and he snicked his secondary membranes over his eyes. Unlike most creatures of the Dark Realm, the redcaps could protect their vision in several degrees of light—even the searing rays of the sun that ruled over the Bright Court. It was part of why the queen preferred the goblins' services above all others.

As he had night after night, Crik found himself in the thinning trees near the edge of a small pond. He crept closer, then took shelter in a stand of rowan and peered through the branches. The sky held the faint luster of pearl here, at the edge of the Dusk Vale, and the water reflected the light back. Carefully he peered through the thin branches, half afraid, half hoping to catch a glimpse of *her*.

And there she was—the water sprite who haunted his dreams. She hovered over the pond she called home, thin and pale, her dragonfly wings brushed with dewdrops.

Crik was not sure what had first drawn him to the place. A certain luminous glow, the sound of her song, the scent of moonlight in the wind. That had been thirteen turnings of the moon ago, and she'd been a deep, bittersweet splinter in his soul ever since.

His knees trembled as he watched her drag one toe through the water, humming. *Beautiful sprite*, he wanted to cry, his heart hot inside his chest, *come dance with me in the gloaming. Lay your long, cool fingers upon my face, and let me drown myself in your eyes.*

But he stayed silent, his breath still. To speak, even to move, would break the spell. She would cry out in horror at the sight of him and flee, and he would lose sight of her forever. It made his heart ache to watch her dip gracefully in and out of the water, wearing it as a shimmering gown, then dashing upward, the luminous spray falling back into the pond like a waterfall.

The thought of frightening her was like a blade slipped under his ribs, and so he remained concealed as always, yearning from afar. She was not for him, and never would be, though sorrow ate him to the bone.

Finally, she tired of her play and plunged beneath the silvered surface of her home. Crik waited for several long minutes, but she did not reemerge.

Footsteps heavy, he made his way back through the dark forest to where the riot snored. By the time he settled back on his mat, he was only able to snatch an hour of restless sleep, disturbed by images of the water sprite, silver and shining in the dusk.

"Up, lazybones." Bonewort's toe in his ribs roused him. "Time to go a'hunting. We've a nice trail to follow."

Crik rubbed the grit from his eyes and sat. He rolled up his mat and stowed it beneath the shrubbery, drank a palmful of cool water from the nearby stream, and was ready to set out with the rest of the raid.

"Here." Bonewort gestured for Crik to join him at the head of the line. "Early to the kill this time, eh youngling?" His yellow eyes glinted.

Crik nodded and took his place behind the leader. His thoughts were cobwebby, and he forced himself to ~~ignore~~ notice the berry bushes they went past, and the silver coins of mushrooms. Hunger growled in his belly.

"We'll feed you up soon enough." Bonewort cuffed his shoulder. "Almost there."

Crik looked up, panic stabbing through him as he recognized the pattern of thinning trees, the faint gray light of the Dusk Vale ahead. They were dangerously near the sprite's pool.

"What do we hunt?" he asked, trying to keep his voice calm.

"Have you ever tasted sprite?" Bonewort's teeth gleamed as he grinned. "Such cool, delicious flesh. Not much blood though, more's the pity. We'll hunt warmer prey after we eat."

Nausea twisted through Crik. "Are you sure this is the right way?" he asked. "The river lies yonder."

He pointed to the left, away from the pond, but the leader shook his head.

"Another time. Today is easy meat."

Crik breathed heavily through his nostrils, mind racing. He had to turn the riot away, but how? He could not fight them all, and he knew of no other prey close by they could be lured to.

There was nothing he could do, except follow Bonewort and desperately hope the sprite was not there. *Where else might she be?* He did not know. Anxiety and revulsion knotted through him until he could barely set one clawed foot in front of the other.

And then they were there, behind the stand of rowans. The faint imprint of his earlier footsteps still showed on the moss, and the bark of one trunk was flayed where his claws had rested. Gulping, Crik turned his gaze away, hoping the other goblins would not notice.

Bonewort held up his hand, and the riot halted. With a nod, they fanned out to encircle the still silver pond.

Crik shot a panicked look at the water, chest heaving. There was no sign of the sprite.

"Nobody there," he whispered.

"Patience," the leader said. "You'll bloody your cap yet."

When the goblins had the pool surrounded, Bonewort let out a sharp whistle. The riot began stomping their feet, making the ferns at the water's edge dip and sway and the rowan branches tremble.

Stay safe, Crik thought fiercely. *Don't come up.*

Too late.

In a spray of silver, the water sprite burst from the surface of her pond. She hovered in midair, droplets sheening her wings. Crik wanted to shout a warning, but his tongue was frozen to his teeth.

With one wide-eyed glance, she took in the redcaps surrounding her. She let out a little gasp and folded her wings, diving for safety, but Bonewort was too clever. His Chasers flung a net across the surface of the water, and her long, pale limbs and shimmering wings were entangled.

She shrieked as they hauled her forth, her dripping fingers gripping the net.

"Help me!" Her gaze went to Crik, those wide, liquid eyes beseeching.

Fire coursed through him, scorching him into action. Taking out his knife, he leaped forward, aiming for the sprite.

Bonewort shouted in approval, then went silent as Crik sliced neatly through the bottom of the net. Quick as a minnow, the sprite slipped down into the water and disappeared.

"What?" The leader rounded on him, anger flaring in his eyes. "What kind of goblin are you, to help our prey escape?"

With trembling claws, Crik tore the cap from his head. "Why must we kill everything that is beautiful and pure? Why?" Loathing for himself, for all his kind, choked him. He threw his cap on the ground and trampled it into the mud. "I renounce my heritage. I give up my place in the tribe."

"You are a stain on redcaps everywhere," Bonewort growled, his eyes a blaze of yellow. "Not even worthy of hauling before the queen. Without your own kind, you are nothing."

Without warning, the big goblin's knife plunged deep between Crik's ribs. Pain came roaring in behind as he fell to his knees. He clutched the hilt of the dagger, his heart's blood pouring in a blackish-red stream over his hands.

The surface of the pond shivered.

Bonewort jerked his blade out, then spat upon Crik's bare head. Eyes narrowed in disgust, he beckoned for the riot to depart.

"Just leave him?" one the Chasers asked.

"He's trash," Bonewort said. "Not even worth gnawing on. He'll be dead soon enough."

As the goblins tramped past, Crik tumbled face-first onto the muddy moss. Then they were gone, and the tangy smell of his own blood filled his senses. The moss was soaked with it, and he was growing cold. So cold.

The dark edges of the forest creaked. The rowan trees rustled. He heard the sound of wood on wood, rough syllables rasped above his head, but they were meaningless.

He had saved his sprite. As the last light dimmed, he wasn't afraid. It had been worth the price.

His heart was fire, then ice, then ashes.

The dryads of the dark oaks surrounded the dying goblin. Their song groaned and whispered around him, the air bitter with the taste of old acorns. With his last breath, the sluggish remains of his blood thickened. His limbs grew, elongating down into the rich soil, stretching up into the dusky air. His hide toughened even further, hardening, drying. Time spun about, a wheel in the sky.

The new moon rose, the shadow of the old moon in her arms. Pale light illuminated the small pond near a stand of rowan trees, the dark forest hunched behind.

On the mossy bank beside the pond, a new tree grew, black and misshapen. Its gnarled branches reached over the water, nearly touching the silvery surface. In the glimmering stillness a water sprite danced, diving in and out of the shadows cast by the tree.

She rose up, wings bejeweled with droplets, and hovered before the twisted trunk for a long moment.

"Thank you," she said, reaching to press a damp hand to the bark.

At her touch, the tree trembled, though there was no wind to stir the branches. From the forest beyond came a low sigh, filled with the scent of night flowers and lost dreams.

With a smile full of sorrow, the sprite gracefully winged back over the center of her pool, her reflection an upside-down twin. She began to dance once more, weaving droplets into a necklace of light, watery gems scattering about her as she whirled.

Under the star-sown sky, the goblin tree kept watch, as it always had... and always would.

Author's Note: Another tale set in the Feyland universe, where magic and mystery reign.

THE TREE OF FATE AND WISHES

THE SOUND of her parent's voices woke Emer Cuinn from dreams filled with blood and ashes. Low and urgent, their conversation penetrated the curtained-off sleeping area of their stone walled dwelling. Emer lay still, straining to hear over the quiet crackle of the peat fire in the main room.

"What did the council say?" Emer's mother asked.

"It's to be war." Her father sounded weary. "Bring my sword and whetstone, Grainne. We march to battle in four days."

Four days? Emer sat up, her heart racing. Yes, the clans often went to war—but it was too soon after their last clash, where her father had been sorely injured. And her bright and laughing cousin, Sean, had been slain—a blade through the chest silencing his merry voice forever.

"Already?" Emer's mother echoed her thoughts. "But Cormac, your wound...you cannot lead the warriors out."

"A chieftain leads his men into battle." His voice was hard.

"But your second in command—"

"Was Sean, and his replacement is still untested. Ask me no more. I'll not shirk my duty."

Careful not to disturb her sleeping siblings, Emer rose, the flagstones cold under her bare feet. Her mother alone could not convince her father, but perhaps he would listen to their combined voices. She wrapped a woolen shawl about her shoulders and pushed open the curtain, blinking in the lantern light. Her mother looked up from the table top, caution and hope in her eyes.

"Please, father," Emer said. "Can the battle not wait?"

Although the deep slice in Cormac's thigh was healing, it had sapped him of much of his strength. On the field of war, that weakness would spell his death.

"Those upstarts graze their cattle upon our summer fields," he said, making a fist upon the table. "Already we've waited too long. We'll drive them off, and add their herds to ours. Which will add to your dowry, lass."

She did not want a dowry bought with the clan's lives. Especially not her father's life.

Emer loved him—loved her whole family—despite the hardness that came upon Cormac when the mantle of chieftain lay heavy upon his shoulders. Her mother, Grainne, trod the balance well between duty and tender care, and her younger brother and sister were the moon and stars to Emer. She could not bear the thought of losing any of them.

"We can move our cattle..." she tried again.

"These are our lands," her father said. "Ours by right of tradition. And force, if need be."

"Go back to bed." Her mother's eyes were sad. There would be no winning the argument that night.

Or any night.

Emer withdrew to the straw-stuffed mattress, but sleep did not come. The clan would go to war in four days. The words echoed in her mind, along with a rising sense of urgency. She must *do* something. But the chieftain's daughter did not have the power to command the clan, however much she might wish it.

Wish...

The thought sparked through her, and with it came a rush of hope. She could not change the course the council had decided upon, but she could invoke the old gods. They had the power to avert the coming war.

Some distance beyond the boundaries of her clan's territory lay a sacred spring. Above the spring a hawthorn tree grew, where for generations people had come to leave their wishes, tied to the branches in the form of cloth strips and long pieces of thread. In all seasons the tree was aflutter with color and movement, the cloth braiding and unbraiding in the wind, the strands dancing in the breeze.

At the wishing tree a girl could perform small magics, beseeching the powers to grant her heart's desire, whether it be love or vengeance or greed. Or peace.

Above the hawthorn tree rose a hill crowned with a circle of standing stones. It was a place of power, and peril. The old gods slept there, and the Fair Folk were known to dance in the ring. Any mortal who offended them brought trouble down upon her head, and upon her entire clan.

One did not go lightly to the wishing tree.

But go she must, for the specter of war panted at her shoulder like a wolfhound, fierce and insatiable, sharp teeth hungry for her father's blood.

The next day, once her chores were finished, Emer told her mother she was going to gather sweet herbs by the waterside.

She did not mention that she wasn't going to the nearby stream, but instead would make for the sacred spring.

"Don't stray too far," her mother said, giving her a stern look.

"I'll be careful." Emer fingered the small dagger strapped at her waist.

She collected her basket and, when her mother's back was turned, slipped an oat cake inside. One must always bring an offering to the gods when making a wish. Then she donned her blue cloak, kissed her brother and sister each upon the cheek, and set out.

At first she kept a decorous pace, but as soon as she was out of sight of the ring fort surrounding their village she gathered up her skirts and ran.

The sun shone down, the morning dew quickly drying from the grasses. The wind off the coast whipped her cloak back. She could not smell the sea—the shore and its tall gray cliffs were too far away—but she felt the weight of the ocean within the breeze.

When she tired, she slowed to catch her breath, then ran once more. She passed the stone cairn marking her clan's boundary and went more warily, though with no less haste. For a time swallows kept her company, darting and turning above her head, but when she came closer to the spring they flew away.

The wind calmed, too, and Emer spotted the weathered circle of stones on the hill above the sacred spring. She veered so she would not come too close to that circle, adjusting her path until the gnarled branches of the hawthorn tree came between her and the hill.

It was in full bloom, the flowers like snow upon the green thorns. Between the drifts of white she spied the colorful tatters of strips tied to the branches. Tens and tens of wishes, left to dance in the wind and flutter beneath the stars, sending their silent prayers into the world.

At the foot of the hawthorn tree the spring lay quiet and dark. A trickle of water wove around root and stone, finally gathering itself into a small stream and meandering away around the base of the hill. The air was thick with power and possibility.

Emer stood a moment, quieting her heavy breaths. She had run far and fast to reach the tree, but it would not do to approach it panting and disheveled. The old gods deserved more than that.

"Caw!"

She started as a raven took flight from the top of the tree. Guardedly, Emer watched it sweep across the sky. One raven was a portent, but not a dire one.

Three ravens, however, meant war.

Stepping carefully, she approached the tree. No more dark shapes stirred in its branches. Still, she felt invisible eyes watching her, the weight of the place folding about her. Sunlight filtered through the hawthorn branches, laying patterns of light and shadow on the grasses.

"Greetings," she said softly. "I come with a peaceful heart to ask a wish."

For a time, she had served as second apprentice to Orla, the clan's wisewoman. From her, Emer had learned a few small bits of magic.

"Magic is action and intent bound together with ritual," Orla had said when Emer asked where the power came from. "Sometimes the gods listen, sometimes they don't. Every one of us holds some power inside, but not everyone is willing to use it."

For this, Emer was willing, though she knew it carried a cost.

She unslung the basket from her arm and drew out the oat cake, then laid her offering upon a flat stone near the spring's edge.

"Please accept this small gift," she said.

Her only answer was the breeze stirring the hanging bits of cloth tied to the thorny branches. Here, beneath the tree, the sweet dusty scent of the flowers filled her nose.

Sitting, Emer worked a length of blue thread free from the hem of her cloak. She snipped it off with her small blade, then brought the thread to her lips and breathed her wish upon the strand. Once, twice, thrice she whispered the words, blowing them against the thread until it was washed in the warmth of her breath.

"Let this war be averted. Let my father grow strong and well. Let us know a time of peace, not bloodshed, between the clans."

She looked up into the tree, finding a spot to tie her wish. Bees hummed among the petals, their song sharpening as they took notice of the large, clumsy human reaching in to disturb their work.

Though she was expecting it, the first sting on her hand made her yelp. Still, she did not withdraw, but looped her string about the dark wood of a small branch.

The second sting, this time on her finger, made her breath hiss between her teeth, but she tied the first knot in the thread.

The third sting was worse than the other two combined, landing in the center of her palm. Eyes blurred with tears, Emer could barely see to wind the thread about itself.

Breathing hard, she finished securing her small magic to the tree.

The moment she let go, the wind lifted the blue strand, and her heart rose at the sight, despite the pain pulsing through her hands.

Perhaps Danu would hear her wish whispering in the breeze. Perhaps the Fair Folk would carry it to the mother goddess's ears. Perhaps all was not lost.

❦

When Emer returned home, hands daubed with mud and a basket full of fresh herbs, her mother gave her a hard look, but said nothing. That evening Emer even had the heart to tease and sing with her siblings before the fire, and went to bed with a spark of hope in her heart.

Her dreams extinguished that spark.

The sky was full of ash, and dead bodies lay strewn upon the trampled grass. She walked among them, too afraid to gaze upon their faces, tears scorching her eyes.

"No." Emer woke with a start, and clutched her blanket up to her chin.

One bit of magic was not enough. She must return to the wishing tree. Two more days, two more chances to strengthen the power of her wish before death came to eat them with its red, insatiable mouth.

I will avert this fate. She put all the force of her soul into the thought, holding it close until morning.

A new day, and warm porridge for breakfast, renewed Emer's resolve.

"Can I check the weirs for trout today?" she asked her mother.

Grainne gave her a long look, but finally nodded. "Keep out of trouble, mind."

"I'm not slipping away to meet with a boy, if that's what you fear."

"Hm." Her mother stirred the pot. "I saw the flowers Young Finn brought you last week."

Emer felt a blush warm her cheeks. "He'd given the same to Cait, the week before. I won't let the likes of Young Finn turn my head."

Though he was a handsome fellow. This last thought, however, her mother did not need to hear.

"Very well—but be home in time for supper. Especially if there's fish."

Emer kissed her mother on the cheek, then went to fetch her cloak and basket. This time, she tucked a small piece of honeycomb in alongside her oat cake.

As she had the day before, as soon as she was out of sight of the ring fort she ran. When she grew too winded she stopped at various points to catch her breath—the hollow where bracken fern grew, the hillock overlooking a rock-strewn plain, the thicket of thorny gorse.

At last she came in sight of the hawthorn tree, the stone circle above standing sentinel. Clouds gathered overhead and the sun slipped behind them. The air suddenly carried a chill.

She paused to smooth her hair and catch her breath. Then, summoning her courage, she proceeded to the dark seep of the spring.

"I ask your indulgence again," she said to the spirits of the place, and to the old gods. "Please accept this offering."

She laid the cake upon the flat stone, and put the honey-comb beside it. Her wish for peace strong within her heart, she unraveled another length of blue thread from her cloak.

"Let this war be averted," she said. "Let my father grow strong and well. Let us know a time of peace between the clans."

The wish welled up from her heart. She could not bear to lose her father as they had lost Sean, now buried beneath the stones. Tears escaped the corners of her eyes, and she caught them upon the thread, letting her sorrow darken the strand.

A soft breeze tickled her cheek, as if in sympathy. Perhaps the gods *were* listening.

When Emer reached up to fasten her wish upon the branch, she drew in a startled breath and froze.

There, beside her first wish, was tied a length of red thread. Fear tickled the back of her neck, and she slowly turned, peering out from the shadows beneath the tree.

Was a warrior of the enemy clan lurking nearby, ready to run her through? Or worse yet, take her hostage?

As if her fright had called it forth, a raven burst from the branches overhead, cawing sharply. Emer's heart pounded like a drum, all her senses shouting at her to run—to abandon her wish and flee back to the safety of her own clan's boundary.

But no. Even if she was about to be taken, she must tie her wish to the tree.

As if from nowhere, a frigid wind sprang up. The air about her turned bitter cold, and Emer's breath plumed out in a white cloud before her face. Her fingers ached as frost swirled around them.

Moving as quickly as she could, she reached to the branch. It took several tries, her numb fingers more like twigs barely under her command than her own flesh, but at last a second blue thread hung beside the first. The cold faded into a warm breeze and her wishes stirred, tangling and twining with the red thread: scarlet like blood, blue like the sky.

What did it mean? She shivered and backed away from the blossom-laden tree. A few petals blew down, dancing away in the wind.

And then she was away, too, running and running until she reached the cairn that marked the boundary of safety. Her hands still ached with a bone-deep cold.

It was growing twilight when she returned home, fingers chapped with cold, four fat trout from the weirs wrapped in leaves and tucked into her basket. Again, her mother gave her a hard look, but did not press.

After supper, Grainne and Cormac spoke of the coming battle, of the readiness of the clan's warriors, of the victory that must surely be theirs.

Emer lay awake, unwilling to fall asleep. When at last she did, ash and blood colored her dreams once more.

When she woke in the light of morning, her throat was clogged with unshed tears. Tomorrow the battle would come.

Almost, she gave up in despair. What good were her feeble wishes against the will of her father and the clan's council?

But stubbornness made her rise, and dress, and once more ask her mother if she might go out, this time to pick nettles.

"I want you close today," Grainne said. "The men are mustering, and the wind tastes of a blade's edge."

"Please." Emer's voice caught on the word. "I must go."

Three was a powerful number, everyone knew that. She must go one more time to the sacred spring, work her small magic, and tie her wish upon the tree.

"No." Her mother shook her head. "I need you to mind your siblings and keep them out from underfoot."

It was a request Emer couldn't refuse. And she would not take her brother and sister with her to the tree. Even if they could keep up, it was far too dangerous, especially with the evidence that someone else had been making their own wishes. Some enemy, wishing for her clan's downfall.

The sun crept across the sky, and Emer tended her siblings and the hearth, starting a rabbit stew and sweeping the floor. Late afternoon skimmed the sky with silver when at last her mother returned from helping provision the warriors.

"You've done well," Grainne said. "You may have your freedom until sunset—but stay close, and be home by dark."

"Thank you." Emer kissed her mother upon the cheek, hoping Grainne hadn't noticed her lack of promises to obey.

She would not be able to reach the sacred spring and make the return journey before twilight lay its shadow over the land. It would be well dark by the time Emer reached home, and she surely would face her mother's wrath, but there was no help for it.

She must make her final wish.

When Grainne wasn't looking, Emer tucked an oat cake into her pouch, along with a small bottle of elderberry wine. She bid farewell to her siblings, summoned a smile for her mother, and slipped out the door.

It seemed the land fought her as she ran—her skirt tangling in the gorse, her shoes sinking into an unexpected bog, thatched clumps of grass making her stumble. At last the hill above the spring rose before her, dark against the dusk-lit sky, the stone circle crouched atop it.

Emer picked the clinging burrs from her skirt and shook it out, then approached the hawthorn tree. A bird rustled in the upper branches, causing a drift of petals, but she could not make out what it was.

Please, not a raven. A third one was proof that the Morrigan, goddess of death and destruction, would bring war to the clan on the morrow.

But war was not a certainty, not yet. Clinging to that handful of hope, Emer laid her oat cake upon the flat stone. She was not sure if she should pour out the bottle of wine as a libation, or leave all the dark liquid within the bottle.

After a moment's hesitation, she unstoppered it and poured a small measure upon the ground, then settled the bottle beside the cake.

"I bring you my small offerings," she said into the oncoming night. "Please grant my wish."

The bird rustled once more among the branches, but still did not take flight and show itself. Afraid of what she would see, she glanced up to where her first two wishes hung.

A second red thread was tied beside her wish from yesterday, and her heart clenched

She stared at the scrap of red fluttering defiantly from the thorny branch. Anger flashed hotly through her. She wanted to turn and shout into the gathering twilight, demand that whoever was there show themselves. How *dare* the enemy come here and tangle their wishes with her own?

She should abandon her foolish hope for peace, and instead use her last wish for her clan's victory in the coming battle.

Emer closed her eyes, her heart torn. The memory of her cousin Sean's death rose within her, searing and futile. It would be easy to draw on that dark, bitter well of emotion, to push it into the magic and turn her hopes from peace to war. The third wish was always the strongest.

Hadn't the interlopers stolen their lands, and even invaded the sacred space of the wishing tree? Perhaps her father was right—the only way to respond was with force. Their warriors were brave and strong. With a heartfelt plea to the Morrigan, surely her clan would prevail.

But victory came with a price. She could not wish for her

father to lie upon the field, dead face staring sightless at the sky.

When she opened her eyes, she saw that the first star had appeared, a speck of light in the ash-gray sky. It was a confirmation of what was in her heart.

Despite the darkest night, there would always be stars.

Tears pricking her eyes even as the star pricked the cloak of the sky, Emer unraveled a final length of blue thread from her hem. This time, after snipping it off, she did not sheathe her small blade. Her first wish had been imbued with her breath, the second her tears. Now it was time for her blood.

Hands steady, she set the tip of the knife against her thumb and pressed until a bright drop welled. Holding her wish close to her heart, she wound the thread about her thumb and let the blood seep in.

"Let this war be averted," she said, the truth of each word ringing from the bottom of her soul. "Let my father become strong again. Let there be peace between the clans."

In the silvery twilight, she reached overhead and fastened her wish to the tree. Her thumb throbbed and the thorns on the branch scored her hands, sharp and biting, as the wishing tree took its own blood sacrifice from her. Emer bit her lip against the pain and finished tying the knot.

The breeze sprang up, pulling the thread from her fingers to dance in the wind, braiding itself with blue, red, blue, red. She withdrew her hands, the backs etched with burning scratches.

Above her, the bird took flight. For a moment all Emer could see was dark feathers, and her heart sank like a stone in deep water. A raven. War and death would fall upon her clan on the morrow.

Then she caught a glimpse of white feathers among the

black. As the bird flew away, the burbling call of a magpie reached her ears. She went to her knees in relief, the dampness soaking through her skirt, but she did not care.

She had done all she could. Now she must make her way home in the dark and face her punishment for disobeying—hard words and a willow cane switching at the least. But if the gods and spirits heard her wish, it was a small price to pay.

Under the pale light of the stars and a sickle moon, she made what haste she could, but it was still two hours after sundown when she at last approached the ring fort.

"Who is it?" The guard at the gate lifted his torch, and she saw that Young Finn was on watch.

"Tis I, Emer," she said wearily. "Let me in."

"Oh, your parents are sore," he said, standing aside. "What have you been up to, out there in the dark?"

He peered into the night, as if expecting to see she'd been keeping company with someone.

"Wishing," she said.

"For victory, I hope!" His smile was white and filled with anticipation. "Tomorrow will be a glorious battle. Give me kiss, for luck."

She brushed her lips against his cheek, but while his heart beat with red blood, hers pulsed with spring water. *Peace, peace.*

When she stepped through the door of their home, she was met with her mother's cold gaze, and her father's face set in anger.

"I know," she said, holding up her poor, abused hands. "I deserve whatever punishment you care to give me. But believe me that I have done what I had to do."

"To bed." Her father pointed to the mattress, where her brother and sister already slept. "Your punishment will come—

but not this night. We must all rest and make ready for tomorrow's battle."

Emer bent her head and hurried to prepare for bed. Whatever befell her clan on the morrow, it was in fate's hands.

⚜

Emer awoke the next morning with no memory of dreams. Predawn light sifted in through the window openings, and she felt the first stirrings of hope.

Then she turned over, and saw her father strapping on his boiled leather breastplate. So. The warriors had not all woken with their desire for battle extinguished.

Surely the gods would act. Her dreams had not carried blood and ash. Did that mean the war was averted?

Quietly, she rose and dressed. She went out and helped her mother serve the men, and few fighting women, mugs of hot herbal brew. Soon after, the warriors were ready, massing at the front gate.

Emer tasted bitter hopelessness.

"I am going with the healers," she told her mother, as the noncombatants prepared to depart with the fighters. When her father fell, she would be there to tend him.

"Emer, what—"

"I am going." She grasped her mother's arms. "I must."

Grainne's dark eyes studied her. Finally she took her daughter's face between her calloused hands.

"Be careful," was all she said, though her expression was full of love and fear and questions that Emer could not answer.

Emer shouldered a pack of supplies and set out along with the healers. In front of them, the younger warriors called cheerfully to one another, while the older men, like her father, went grimly forward. They, at least, knew that battles brought death as well as glory.

Too soon they reached the field where the chieftains had agreed to meet. The sun had risen and clawed away the mist shrouding its face. It was too beautiful a morning for death, and Emer swallowed back the salt of her tears.

At least she would be there to bear witness as her clansmen fell. Her heart hardened against the gods as she saw the black line of opposing warriors waiting across the field. There would be no peace.

Grief aching through her body, Emer set down the pack she'd been carrying. Despite herself, her feet carried her forward until she stood at the front lines.

"Get back," Young Finn told her, with a fierce look.

Then the war pipes began to play, wailing loud as though giving voice to her anguish. Across the field, Emer glimpsed a red cloak.

No.

She did not realize she was screaming the word as she sprinted forward. Open sky and green grass lay before her; and the faces of her enemies. Dimly, she was aware of a handful of warriors following behind her.

The opposing clan stirred, a group of them also moving onto the field.

"Come back!" her father called, but she could not.

There, as if in a mirror, a dark-haired girl in a red cloak ran across the field toward Emer, her face full of sorrow, full of hope. Behind her came her clan's warriors, until they were halted by a sharp command from their chieftain.

Closer Emer came to the stranger girl, closer, and closer still, until they met in the middle of the field.

"You," Emer gasped out. "You were wishing. Tell me—tell me what your wish was."

"I wished for peace," the other girl said. "My name is Dierdre."

"I am Emer, and I wished the same." She could not keep a tear from slipping down her face.

"Well met, friend." Dierdre held out her hands.

They were welted with bee stings, chapped with cold, covered with scratches.

Emer stepped forward and clasped Dierdre's hands.

"Yes," was all she said.

They embraced then, and the breeze danced about them, whipping their cloaks together, red and blue.

Behind each of them, the warriors stilled and whispered. The chieftains waved their men back. Each one strode to the center of the field where their wayward daughters stood, hair tangling together, faces bright with hope.

There would be no war today.

Nor was there, not for generations. Not until the last of the red thread and the blue thread frayed and faded and finally let go, whirling away from the tree into a night filled with wind, and stars, and the memory of two girls standing arm-in-arm against the tide.

❦

Author's Note: As a fan of Celtic legend, I wanted to weave in the history of the Wishing Trees still present all over Ireland. This tale is set in the same ancient Celtic world as my stories *Fae Horse* and *Beneath the Knowe*.

OTHER WORKS

THE FEYLAND SERIES

What if a high-tech game was a gateway to the treacherous Realm of Faerie?

THE FIRST ADVENTURE - Book 0 (prequel)

THE DARK REALM – Book 1

THE BRIGHT COURT – Book 2

THE TWILIGHT KINGDOM – Book 3

FAERIE SWAP - Book 3.5

TRINKET (short story)

SPARK - Book 4

BREAS'S TALE - Book 4.5

ROYAL - Book 5

MARNY - Book 6

CHRONICLE WORLDS: FEYLAND

FEYLAND TALES: Volume 1

VICTORIA ETERNAL

Steampunk meets Space Opera in a British Galactic Empire that never was...

PASSAGE OUT

STAR COMPASS

STARS & STEAM

COMETS & CORSETS

THE DARKWOOD CHRONICLES

*Deep in the Darkwood, a magical doorway leads to the enchanted and
dangerous land of the Dark Elves-*

ELFHAME

HAWTHORNE

RAINE

SHORT STORY COLLECTIONS

TALES OF FEYLAND & FAERIE

TALES OF MUSIC & MAGIC

THE FAERIE GIRL & OTHER TALES

THE PERFECT PERFUME & OTHER TALES

COFFEE & CHANGE

MERMAID SONG

ABOUT THE AUTHOR

Growing up, Anthea Sharp spent most of her summers raiding the library shelves and reading, especially fantasy. She now makes her home in the Pacific Northwest, where she writes, plays the fiddle, hangs out in virtual worlds, and spends time with her small-but-good family. Contact her at antheasharp@hotmail.com or visit her website – www.antheasharp.com and join her new release mailing list (plus get a bonus free story when you sign up!)

Anthea also writes historical romance under the pen name Anthea Lawson. Find out about her acclaimed Victorian romantic adventures at www.anthealawson.com.